JOHN
AND THE
JESUS BOAT
EPISODE THREE

ROLIN
BRUNO

AD 29–ELIJAH'S MOUNTAIN

STONEWALL PRESS
PAVING YOUR WAY TO SUCCESS

Printed in the United States of America

ISBN: 978-1-64460-136-5 (Paperback)
ISBN: 978-1-64460-135-8 (eBook)

Library of Congress Control Number: 2019933363

Stonewall Press
363 Paladium Court
Owings Mills, MD 21117
www.stonewallpress.com
1-888-334-0980

ABOUT THE COVER

Capernaum Synagogue

The cover image shows the remains of the synagogue in Capernaum, Galilee. It was in operation during the first century AD, and was rebuilt in the fourth century AD.

Jesus moved from Nazareth to Capernaum when he began his ministry. Here at the synagogue is where Jesus stood to deliver many of his teachings. The Jewish populace there was generally receptive to Jesus. In Capernaum Jesus healed the dying son of a government official (John 4:46-54), the injured servant of a Roman Centurion (Matthew 8:5-13), and raised the dead daughter of Jairus, a ruler of this synagogue (Mark 5:21-24, 35-43). In this synagogue Jesus cast out a demon for the first time, from one of the men attending.

Although Jerusalem sent representatives to attack Jesus' message in Capernaum, it is not surprising that Jesus came under little persecution from the rulers and inhabitants in this city.

About the Author

Rolin Bruno is a Bible scholar and street evangelist with a vivid imagination that fills the gaps in Bible stories.

He has served as pastor at a storefront church on Skid Row in Los Angeles and as a street evangelist in the cities of Southern California, Western Pennsylvania, and the Gulf Coast of Mississippi.

Rolin has a calling to serve the homeless. In Louisiana and Mississippi he served as a home missionary to stricken residents after the devastation of Hurricane Katrina, teaching spiritual disciplines and twelve-step recovery from addictions. In Pennsylvania, he served as a street evangelist to pre-teen street kids, and helped lead them through the Youth Alpha program to answer their questions about God and Jesus.

Rolin is a 2003 graduate of Vanguard University of Southern California, studying religion and ministry. He continued at Vanguard to earn a Master's degree in religion and Bible. His 2006 master's thesis is on the letter of Jude, "Jude and the Scoffers." This 278-page opus is available for purchase at http://www.tren.com.

He is an ordained deacon of the Communion of Evangelical Episcopal Churches and of the Anglican Communion in North America, and has a heart for planting new chapters of Celebrate Recovery.

Rolin lives in the mountains of Southern California and is an avid camper and backpacker. He has hiked the Grand Canyon, Mount Whitney, the Inyo Mountains, and 570 miles of the Pacific Crest Trail.

CONTENTS

Prologue

Garbage Heap

Thursday 6 January AD 29, 9:00 AM

"David! Dan! Help me with this!"

The two boys came over to where Hezekiah was standing in smoky haze atop the trash heap at the bottom of the Hinnom Valley, also known as the cursed Gehenna.[1] They were doing their morning walk looking for things that they could sell. David was nine years old now and Dan was eight, so their mother Abigail let them go with their eleven-year-old brother on these scavenger runs.

David asked, "What'd you find, Hezzy?"

"Look at this heavy-duty rope! I bet we could sell it for a half-shekel. But it's stuck under this dead donkey."

"Yeah, but it stinks. Nobody would buy that."

"Oh yes, we can wash it off in the Brook Kidron. There's lots of water over there right now."

David and Dan grabbed the rope with their brother and they swung their weight down the trash-heap. The rope burst loose from under the donkey and the three boys tumbled onto each other laughing.

David said, "Hey, this rope is slimy."

Dan said, "Eww! Maggots!" He dropped the rope. "Don't these maggots ever die?"

"It's okay," said Hezekiah. "I can drag it from the clean end." He looked up from what he was doing, and over Dan's shoulder he recognized someone coming down the hill from the Essene Gate in the Jerusalem wall.

Hezzy called out, "John! Over here! Good to see you!"

John picked his way through the rubbish heaps to where the three boys stood. "Hi, guys! What's all this smoke here?"

"It's been burning all year," said Hezekiah. "I think somebody camped here and their fire got away from them. They sent Roman soldiers to put it out, but it just starts up again. It's burning deep underground. What brings you to Jerusalem, John?"

"Jesus sent twelve of us out to take his message to the cities and towns in Judea. But right now we're visiting in Jerusalem to celebrate the Festival of Lights.[2]

"Wanna come with us to the temple tonight to watch 'em light the second candle? You could wear your best tunic, the one with no seams."

"Oh, I had to sell that. I found out that the Thieves Guild was planning to kill me so they could steal it."

"Oh, that's too bad, Hezzy. But the three of you can eat with us tonight. We're staying at Martha and Mary's house in Bethany. They're longtime friends of Jesus."

"I'll ask my mom. She'll say yes for sure."

1

Band on the Run

SUNDAY 9 JANUARY AD 29, 1:00 PM

John went to answer the knock on the door at Martha and Mary's house. Four young men were standing outside, two of whom John knew quite well.

"Daniel! Linus! What a surprise! Come on in!" John shut the door behind the four men.

Daniel said, "John, you remember Libni and his cousin Shimei here, don't you?"

"Yes I sure do. You guys were all disciples of John the Baptist with me. Welcome! But how'd you find us? Nobody's supposed to know we're here."

Daniel said, "It took us a bit to find you. We finally went asking at the Synagogue of David, and the rabbi sent us to a boy named Hezekiah. Hezekiah sent us here."

John said, "Well, what's going on, guys? This must be something important!"

Daniel said, "I'm afraid so, John. Four days ago, King Herod killed our prophet, John the Baptist."

John felt like he'd been punched in the stomach. "Oh, no! I'm—I'm so sorry, guys! He was my friend, too."

Linus said, "Herod chopped off the prophet's head. We heard about it from the jailer the next day, and he let us come take the body. We buried him just before Sabbath. But that's not all. It gets worse."

"What could be worse?" said John.

Daniel said, "Word on the street is that Herod wants to finish the job by chopping the heads off all the prophet's disciples, beginning with the most famous one."

"Well, you guys aren't famous. Who's he talking about?"

"It's said that Herod wants to give his wife a present—the head of Jesus of Nazareth on a platter."

John was shocked and confused. "Oh, mercy. This is awful! What are we gonna do now?"

"We don't know," said Daniel. "We came to talk with you guys about it."

"Come and sit down, guys," said John. "This is a shock." He led them to a room with a low dining table and they sat on the cushions there. He brought them some dates to munch on.

John said, "There's nobody here but Andrew and me right now. He'll be right back. The others went on a walk to see the Mount of Olives. Where have you guys been?"

Linus said, "We were afraid, so we left Herod's territory in Perea and came to Anathoth, here in the Roman governor's territory. Anathoth is Libni and Shimei's hometown, and we figured we could hide out there."

Libni said, "Nobody ever bothers us in little Anathoth. We only have twenty houses in the whole town."

Shimei said, "But when we got there we found out that two of Jesus' disciples had been there for a week and left there to go celebrate the Festival of Lights. So we came looking for you guys to warn you about the news."

John said, "What about the rest of the Baptist's disciples? Where are they gonna go?"

Linus said, "The other four disciples want to keep baptizing and spreading Prophet John's message. Some of the

people he baptized asked us to come visit their hometowns. So the other four have an invitation to cross the Great Sea to live in Ephesus. They're on their way to Caesarea to see if they can find a ship and get out of the country."

Daniel said, "Yes, but the four of us want to follow Jesus of Nazareth, the one who is greater than Prophet John."

John said, "But Jesus is in danger too. He's been living in Capernaum, and Herod Antipas is the king there also."

"This is really messed up," said Linus.

"That's for sure," said John. "Let's get together with the rest of the Twelve when they get back, and see what we can figure out. I wish Jesus were here."

Mary and her brother Lazarus were helping Martha prepare an afternoon snack for their sixteen guests. The Twelve were in the dining area listening to the four disciples of the Baptist tell their story. Everyone was upset at the news that Jesus' life had been threatened.

Nathanael said, "How do we know this is true? Maybe it's just another one of those rumors that spread around in the streets."

Daniel said, "I first heard it from the jailer at Herod's castle in Machaerus.[3] He said he heard it from his wife. His wife said she heard Queen Herodias herself say that King Herod was going to deliver Jesus' head on a platter to her."

"That's not good," said Matthew. "Still, we have some followers of Jesus who are well-placed in Herod's service. They should be able to confirm or deny whether this is true or not. But it may take some time."

Peter's brother Andrew said, "John and I have a friend in Jerusalem: Elnathan, a disciple of Nicodemus. We can find out from him whether the Supreme Council knows anything about this."

Simon Peter said, "I think it would be best for us to go back to Capernaum and consult with Jesus."

John's brother "Big" James said, "Peter, you're right. We need to be near Jesus to guard against assassins."

Simon the Zealot said, "But Jesus sent us out to spread the good news of the kingdom of God."

Matthew's brother James Alpheus said, "Yes, but he didn't tell us how long to stay out here. And we've already accomplished each of the things Jesus told us to do."

"That's true," said Thomas. "But Jesus is also fishing for men, somewhere in northern Galilee. We don't know if he's come back to Capernaum yet."

Philip said, "If he's not there, we can send out messengers to track him down in Galilee. We'll find him."

"I'm scared," said Judas Thaddeus.

"Don't be afraid, Tad," said Judas of Kerioth. "Jesus has enough power to protect all of us."

"Okay, it's settled," said Peter. "We can slip out with the crowds right after they light the fifth candle at the Festival of Lights tonight. That'll give John and Andrew time to find Elnathan and see if he knows anything. We can travel by night till we get to the Alpheus house in Ephraim."

Andrew said, "Daniel, it's your choice: you four can either hide out in Anathoth or come along with us to find Jesus."

"We're coming with you guys," said Daniel. "There's no future for us in Anathoth."

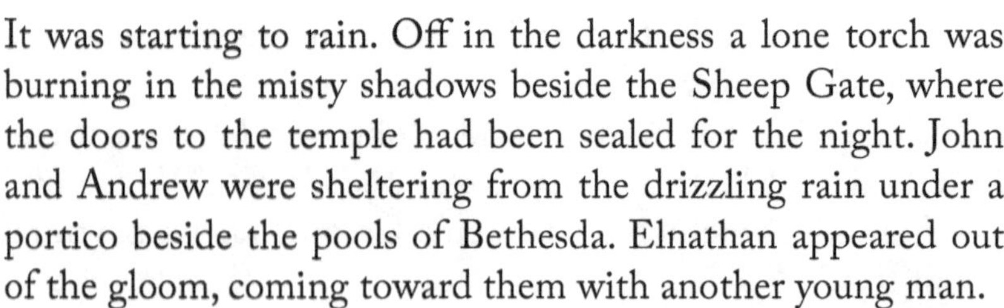

It was starting to rain. Off in the darkness a lone torch was burning in the misty shadows beside the Sheep Gate, where the doors to the temple had been sealed for the night. John and Andrew were sheltering from the drizzling rain under a portico beside the pools of Bethesda. Elnathan appeared out of the gloom, coming toward them with another young man.

Elnathan said, "Hi, guys. This is Clopas. He's a disciple of Nicodemus like me. Clopas, this is John and Andrew."

John said, "Hi, Clopas. What'd you find out, Elnathan?"

"I talked with Nicodemus. He said they don't know any more than you do about Herod's threat. The high priests have heard the rumor but they don't know if it's real yet. They're waiting to see if any news develops on this."

"Well at least they're not looking for us," said Andrew. "But this situation is only a few days old. It would be nice for us to have an information contact in Jerusalem."

Clopas said, "That's the same thing Nicodemus said."

John said, "Elnathan, is he going to let you become a disciple of Jesus like you wanted?"

"Yes, and the same for Clopas. Clopas has listened to Jesus teaching and wants to be one of his disciples also. But Nicodemus advised the two of us to stay in Jerusalem so we can take messages to you guys in Galilee about the dangers that are developing."

Andrew said, "There's more than one danger?"

Elnathan said, "Yes. Caiaphas the high priest was upset about what happened after Jesus was accused of drinking blood. The Supreme Council brought in both of the witnesses and examined them separately. Caiaphas got angry because their testimonies didn't agree."

"Yes, we heard about that," said Andrew.

"But there's more. Now Caiaphas is paying three young Pharisees to shadow Jesus to see if they can catch him in something he says. The high priests in the Supreme Council want to put him on trial. They say he's a trouble-maker."

John said, "Hey, we've seen those three guys! Nathanael found out their names: Terah, Talmon, and Temeni. They're all related to each other."

"Yes. They were trying to catch up to Jesus in Galilee. They followed some of his disciples back to Judea, but Jesus wasn't with them. So, they came back to Caiaphas and he sent them to Capernaum to wait for Jesus."

"That's funny," said Andrew. "They followed us south, but Jesus went north."

Clopas said, "One more piece of news, but this is good news instead of bad."

"Oh, what?" said John.

"Nicodemus heard about the time Jesus was teaching in Chorazin and people had to stand outside because the synagogue was too small. Now Nicodemus is going to pay to have a full-sized marble synagogue built there, so the workers on his farmlands will have enough room for their Sabbath services."

"Well, that's good. Thanks for all this news, guys," said Andrew.

John said, "Clopas, welcome to our band. But we gotta get out of here. The rest of the gang is waiting outside Jerusalem for us."

Clopas said, "Yeah, you'd better get going. Right now, you guys are rabbits on the run."

2

ANXIOUS FOR NOTHING

FRIDAY, 14 JANUARY AD 29, 3:30 PM

"Daddy's coming! Daddy's coming!" Matthew's sons Amram and Izhar ran off shouting excitedly after hugging their father. They were taking the news of his return to their mother and sister and their two younger brothers.

Matthew said, "Well, so much for a quiet arrival. Now the whole town will know we're here."

The sixteen tired followers of Jesus were walking up the street to Matthew's house in Capernaum. Simon Peter had just rejoined them, returning from a side trip to his own house to talk with his mother-in-law Perpetua.

Andrew said, "Hey Bro, did you find out anything?"

Peter said, "Yes. Jesus isn't back yet, but he sent Perez ahead with instructions for us. He's at Matthew's house waiting for us. Perpetua said Jesus is travelling in from the north and will be teaching at the Chorazin synagogue tonight."

"Oh, wow," said John. "Should we go up there to meet him? We could get there in an hour or so."

"Yes, but Sabbath is at hand and we haven't set up lodging there," said Peter. "Let's wait to see what Perez has for us."

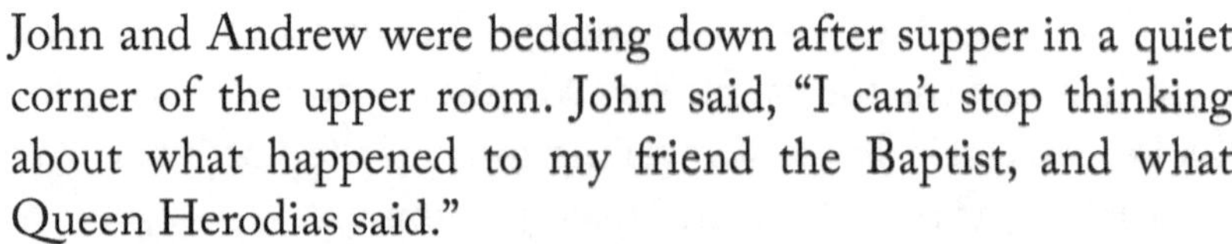

Matthew's wife Paula was leaving with her daughter Sarah to borrow some food for her new guests from her friend Portia, the mayor's wife. Amram was leading his three younger brothers in a quiet game in another room. The Twelve and the four disciples of the Baptist were gathering in Matthew's large upper room to hear from Perez, who had been traveling with Jesus.

"Welcome home, men," said Perez. "We thought you might be arriving back from your missions two by two. But here you are all together! Jesus sent me ahead with instructions for you."

"We're all ears," said Peter. "Is it complicated?"

"No, it's really simple. Jesus wants you to take this time to rest and relax, to stay at Matthew's house for now and refresh yourselves, and be anxious for nothing."

"But we heard bad news," said Thaddeus.

"Matthew told me about that, and I'm on my way to Tiberias to ask my friend Chuza about those rumors." said Perez. "Chuza manages Herod's private land holdings, and he might know something. But the Master wants you to put your minds at ease and rest. Jesus will be back in Capernaum before next Sabbath to listen to your stories."

John and Andrew were bedding down after supper in a quiet corner of the upper room. John said, "I can't stop thinking about what happened to my friend the Baptist, and what Queen Herodias said."

"I have an idea," said Andrew. "We can think about all the things we did when we were out spreading the good news."

"That's a great idea."

"Yes, and I can't wait to tell Jesus all about it."

3

TELL THAT FOX

SUNDAY, 16 JANUARY AD 29, 11:00 AM

"Jesus is coming! Jesus is coming!" It was Amram and Izhar again, running up the road from the lake and shouting.

John got up from where he had been lounging under one of the olive trees outside the gate of Matthew's house. "Hi guys! Where'd you see Jesus?"

Izhar said, "He just got to the edge of the city, right where my dad used to run his tax collector's booth."

Amram said, "He's coming real slow, 'cause there's a big crowd around him that wants to see him."

"Well, go on inside and tell everyone to come out," said John. "We can give him a big welcome right here."

The Twelve gathered in the small olive orchard around Matthew's house, along with Matthew's family. Perez wasn't there, for he hadn't yet returned from Tiberias.

Judas Thaddeus said, "The whole city will know that Jesus is here now. We won't be safe in this town."

"You're right, Tad," said Philip.

"I wouldn't be so sure of that, guys," said Andrew. "Matthew's friend Jaroel is the mayor, and Jesus healed Jaroel's little son who was dying.[4] Jesus has been under protection from the mayor ever since then."

"Yes, and Jaroel is a royal official, a nobleman," said Simon the Zealot. "The blood of the family of Herod the Great runs in his veins. He could put up a fuss against Antipas."

John said, "And Claudius, the centurion of the Roman garrison here in Capernaum is on Jesus' side too. Jesus healed a servant of Claudius at his request, a man he valued highly.[5] I don't think we'll have any trouble from the Romans."

"Well, we do know that the high priest in Jerusalem wants to kill Jesus," said Thaddeus.

Big James said, "Yes, he sent three Pharisees here to try to find some crime to charge against him. But they're getting no cooperation from the synagogue, ever since Jesus raised Jairus' twelve-year-old daughter from the dead.[6] Jairus is a top official of the Capernaum synagogue."

Nathanael said, "I wouldn't put much trust in what the family of Herod might do. They're famous for conspiring against one another. Herod the Great even killed some of his own sons. And the Pharisees in Jerusalem are still plotting against Jesus."

Thomas said, "Yes, but they're eighty-five miles away from us, and King Herod is at least a hundred miles away."

"Well, Herod will be here at Tiberias in the spring," said Simon the Zealot, "and we don't know what he's going to do."

"Jesus will know what to do," said Judas of Kerioth. "Maybe it's time for him to call up an army."

James the Levite, father of Thaddeus, said, "Hey look, here come some Pharisees down the road from above!"

Nathanael said, "It's the same three! Hi, Terah! Hi, Talmon and Temeni! What brings you here?

"We bring a word for Jesus of Nazareth." Said Terah.

"Well, you can give it to him right away," said Nathanael. "Here he comes up the road now."

The fifteen disciples who had been travelling with Jesus in northern Galilee were at the forefront of the crowd, followed by Jesus. He in turn was being followed by several dozen locals from Capernaum.

Peter spotted his wife near the front of the crowd. He shouted, "Concordia!" and ran down to meet her, sweeping her up into his arms. He picked her up and carried her up the street.

Peter set Concordia down in front of Matthew's house. Her cheeks were flushed with excitement. Jesus arrived shortly behind them.

Peter said to Jesus, "Master, it's so good to see you!"

"Yes, Peter, and it's good to see my Twelve again! I can't wait to hear of all the victories you have had, spreading the good news in Judea. Come! Let's go inside and tell tales!"[7]

The three Pharisees were sidling up, trying to get near. Jesus said, "Ah, here are my three faithful Pharisees! I have missed you. What word do you have for me today?"

Terah said, "We came to tell you to leave this place, and go away, for Herod wants to kill you."

Jesus said, "Go and tell that fox, 'Look! I'm casting out demons and performing cures today and tomorrow, and the third day I will reach my goal.' Nonetheless, I must continue journeying today and tomorrow and the next, for it cannot be that a prophet should perish outside of Jerusalem."[8] And Jesus turned from them and entered the house with his disciples.

4

• •

SEND IN THE WOMEN

MONDAY, 17 JANUARY AD 29, 9:00 AM

John, Andrew, and Nathanael were in the kitchen of Matthew's house along with Matthew and his wife Paula. They were warming themselves after breakfast by the kitchen fire, for it was cold outside and had started to rain.

Jesus had gone already, taking the four disciples of John the Baptist with him. He was spending the whole day with them at Peter's house, teaching them and comforting them over the death of their leader.

Perez appeared at the kitchen door. Matthew said, "Hi, Perez, welcome back! Hey, you're dripping wet! Come closer to the fire and warm up!"

"Yes, this rain caught me by surprise," said Perez. "I just got back from Tiberias. I had a chance to talk to Chuza about that rumor going around."

"Did you find out anything?"

Perez said, "Not much at all. Herod's been in a nasty mood ever since he ordered the killing of the Baptist. The whole staff at Machaerus is afraid to talk to him about it, or even mention it. Chuza heard this from a servant who came back from Herod's birthday party."

Andrew said, "So we don't know if it's safe to stay here in Capernaum, then."

"Herod will spend this winter at Machaerus beside the desert," said Perez. "But he'll be returning here to Tiberias in the spring. I'll be able to find out more detail then."

"That doesn't make me feel better at all," said John.

Paula had been listening to all of this. She broke in, saying, "What is this you men have been up to? What rumor is this?"

Nathanael said, "Ever since Herod killed John the Baptist, the word on the street is that he wants to kill Jesus also, as the most notable disciple of the Baptist."

"That's an interesting rumor. But you're doing this all wrong. If you want to find out the truth about such things, you have to send in the women, not the men. I will find out about this for you."

John said, "That's cool, miss Paula! How will you find out?"

Paula said, "You're forgetting that mayor Jaroel and his wife Portia were invited to Herod's birthday party, and they've already returned home. Portia spent her time at the party with the other women, and even saw Queen Herodias. I'll have the answer for you by tonight."

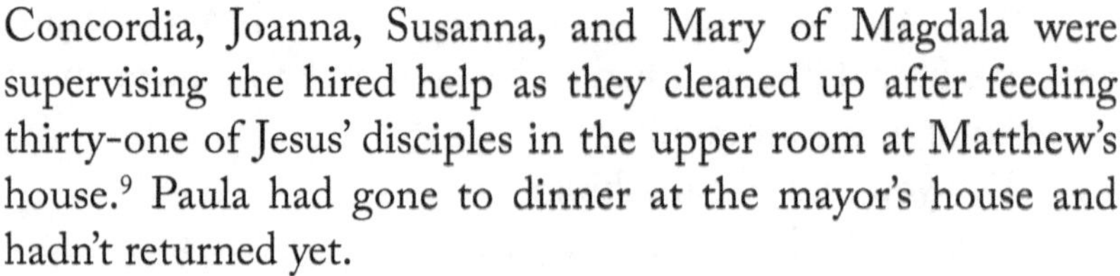

Concordia, Joanna, Susanna, and Mary of Magdala were supervising the hired help as they cleaned up after feeding thirty-one of Jesus' disciples in the upper room at Matthew's house.[9] Paula had gone to dinner at the mayor's house and hadn't returned yet.

John and Thaddeus were waiting near the gate for Paula to come back, hoping to hear some news, when she knocked on the gate. John opened it and Paula entered while he barred it behind her.

John said, "Hi, Miss Paula. Did you find out anything?"

"Yes, John, I sure did," said Paula. "The entire rumor is a false alarm and was never true."

"Wow," said John. "How did it ever get started?"

"Queen Herodias started it herself, and she would really like for it to be true. But Herod is furious with her for maneuvering him into killing the Baptist, and he won't even let his queen come in to see him right now. There's no chance that she could get him to kill another prophet, after what happened with the first one."

Judas Thaddeus said, "Neat! So, we don't have to worry. Jesus is safe and so are we."

"Not so fast. Herod was fascinated by the Baptist, and used to go down into the dungeon to talk with him. Now he's fascinated by this Jesus he's hearing about."

"I don't know whether that's good or bad," said John.

"Probably not good," said Paula. "Some people are telling him that Jesus is now the Baptist raised from the dead, and Antipas is afraid the Baptist has come back to haunt him. He wants to see this new prophet Jesus, as he calls him. But he hasn't given orders to capture Jesus, and no one knows if he'll actually try to arrest him." [10]

"Oh, shoot," said Thaddeus.

"Come on," said John, "let's go tell the others!"

5

· ·

NO TIME TO EAT

John came down from the upper room at Matthew's house looking for his friend Matt, Matthew's oldest son. He found him in the kitchen with his sister Sarah, waiting for breakfast.

John said, "Hey Matt! Wanna go with me to Peter's house real quick? I gotta get one of Jesus' scrolls for him, and bring back some Sabbath bread. Jesus' mom just got back from Cana and she helped bake a big batch yesterday."

"Sure, I'll go! Jesus' mom and Concordia's mom both make great bread."

"That's what I was thinking," said John. "We can snack on the way back."

Sarah said, "Hey, I wanna go too! Besides, if they made enough bread for everyone you'll need my help."

The three went out into the courtyard, where they heard a knocking at the gate. Matt opened it, and found seven men and women standing outside. One of them said, "Hey, here's two of Jesus' disciples! Young men, can you get us in to see Jesus? I need a special healing, and so do some of the rest of us."

John said, "This is not the time to disturb the Master right now. He's going to be reading the *haftarah*[11] at synagogue in two hours. You should wait for him after the service."

The seven supplicants looked crestfallen, and wanted to argue with John, but he hurried down the street with Matt.

Matt said, "What scroll does Jesus want? They have most all the books of the prophets at the synagogue already."

John said, "I know, but he wanted his own scroll. I'm getting the Book of Samuel. Something about David going out to war."

"It's almost like going out to war lately for us, just to get out the front gate. Everybody's asking for healing or something and we barely have time to eat," said Matt.

"Jesus said you guys are supposed to be resting up and relaxing, but that's not happening," said Sarah.

"Maybe today will be better," said Matt.

------- •◦●◦●◦●◦•• -------

Jesus stood up to read, and John handed him the Book of Samuel. He rolled it open to near the end, and began to read:

> Once upon a time there was war between Israel and the Philistines. King David led his men out to battle, but as he fought the Philistines he became exhausted. Then the Philistine Benob, a descendant of the giants, took David prisoner and was about to kill him. Benob's bronze spear weighed three hundred shekels. But Abishai son of Zeruiah came to David's rescue, striking the Philistine down and killing him.
>
> After that David's officers took an oath before King David, saying, "Never again shall you go out with us to war, for fear that the Lamp of Israel might be extinguished." [12]

Jesus handed the scroll back to John and sat down. There was a brief moment of silence in the packed-out synagogue before Jesus began to speak.

He proclaimed loudly, "Where can you find the Lamp of Israel? You have gone to see John the Baptist, and heard him testify to the truth. His was a lamp that was burning, and shining brightly, and you all were willing to rejoice for a while in its light.[13]

"John the Baptist was sent by God, and came as a witness to testify about the Light, so that all might believe through him. For the true Light has come into the world, to enlighten every man and woman. The Light is in the world, but the world does not know him. He has come to his own, but his own have not received him.

"The true Light dwells among you. He is the one of whom the Baptist said, 'He who comes after me has a higher rank than I, for he existed before me.'

"As many as do receive the Light, to them he is giving the right to become children of God. Those who believe in his name are not born of blood, nor of the will of the flesh, nor of the will of man, but of the will of God.[14]

"He who has ears, let him hear. She who has ears, let her hear." Jesus stopped speaking, and a murmur rolled through the crowd. The elders continued with the synagogue service.

John and Andrew stepped out the synagogue door, and immediately a man limped up to them. He said, "Are you some of the Twelve who were commissioned by Jesus?"

John said, "Yes we are. Why do you ask?"

"Dear sirs, I was working last week helping some house-builders, and a beam dropped on my ankle and injured me. I am in great pain, and I can't work and earn a living while I have this pain. Will you help me?"

Andrew said, "Stretch out your leg." The man did so. John and Andrew laid their hands on his leg and began praying that the man would be healed and relieved of pain in the name of Jesus, while the rest of the people from the synagogue streamed out around them.

After a few minutes the man said, "The pain is gone! Thank you, honorable sirs. I can go back to work tomorrow!"

While he was saying this, Thaddeus and his father James were descending the steps of the synagogue as another man led a young girl by the hand up toward them. But before the man could speak, an unclean spirit in the girl called out loudly, "I know who you are! You are disciples of the Son of God! What do you want with us?" Tad and his dad commanded the spirit to be quiet and to depart in the name of Jesus. Instantly the girl was released from the unclean spirit.

Similar things were happening all around John and Andrew, with people requesting to be healed. One man approached Nathanael's cousin Matthias. Matthias said, "I haven't been given authority to help you. Here is Nathanael son of Tholmai.[15] He's one of the Twelve; ask him."

The three Pharisees who had been sent to monitor Jesus stood off to the side, fuming. They were watching all this "work" being performed on the Sabbath, and they could do nothing about it.

———————— •••••• ————————

The sun had set behind the hills to the west of Capernaum, but Jesus with his disciples had not yet reached Matthew's house. Jesus was attending to every person that came up to him for a blessing or a healing or just an encouragement, and was only able to move a few feet at a time toward the house.

At long last they reached the house, and Matt barred the gate behind them. Jesus went up the stairs to the upper room, beckoning his disciples to follow him. They found the low table there already set with food and drink.

Jesus reclined by the table and drank from a cup of wine, first saying, "Blessed are you Lord God, King of the Universe, who brings forth the fruit of the vine." Then he took a piece of bread and raised it, saying, "Blessed are you Lord God, King of the Universe, who brings forth bread from the earth."

John sat down on the floor beside him. From hearing Jesus say the blessing, he could tell that his Master was exhausted. Jesus ate a few more bites and took another drink of wine, then lay his head on John's lap.

John looked down at Jesus, and was startled to see that he had fallen fast asleep. He looked around the room and made eye contact with Andrew, who had seen what was happening. Andrew went to get a cushion and gave it to John.

John took a few bites of food himself, then finished the wine that was left in Jesus' cup. He leaned back on the cushion and closed his eyes for just a few seconds. But that was the last John remembered of that night.

6

. . . .

NIGHT MOVES

John felt someone squeeze his shoulder, and he opened his eyes. It was Jesus, getting ready to go out to pray. Food and drink were still on the table from last night, and the dishes hadn't been cleared. There were men sleeping all over the room, most of them on their pallets but a few of them right next to the table, along with Jesus and John.

John got up and silently followed Jesus down the stairs and out the door. Without a word, they walked through the deserted streets and up into the hills overlooking Capernaum. Jesus stopped at a hilltop and motioned for John to stay, then he walked about a stone's throw away and began to pray.

Jesus was on his knees, bent over with his face toward the ground. John knelt and began to pray also. He started by asking God to wake him up and clear his mind.

———•••●••———

The sun was beginning to peek over the heights of Golan on the other side of the lake when Jesus came back to John, who was watching the sun rise. Jesus said, "Find Beon and Bohan and send them to Bethsaida to bring your dad 'Big Thunder' to Capernaum with his boat. We will be needing some transportation. And tell Peter to have all the disciples gather in the upper room after the morning meal, for I have a word for them."

"Yes, Teacher," John replied. "Should Beon and Bohan wait until you talk to the disciples before they leave?"

"No, I will speak with them when they get back. I would like to see your Father with his boat before nightfall."

John was puzzled by this, but he set off down the hill without asking, leaving Jesus behind.

Jesus walked into the upper room with Peter behind him. The men and women there had just finished their morning meal. All eyes were on Jesus as he began to speak.

"Dearly beloved, it is time for a winter's rest. I am releasing you to go to your homes and families. For those of you who have left your homes for my sake, lodging will be found for you in Bethsaida. We will gather all the disciples together again in the early spring, and continue that mission that the Father has assigned for me.

"As for the Twelve I set aside to be with me, come away by yourselves to the wilderness with me and rest a while.[16] We will leave by boat tonight after dark, so that we will not be followed.

"Simon Peter has detailed instructions for you. And for all of you, be of good cheer, for after this night, and another day and another night, my journey will come to the fulfillment spoken by the prophets about me."

Jesus went downstairs to eat in the kitchen while some of the disciples sat in stunned silence, and yet others began talking freely.

Simon Peter called them to attention. "Brothers and sisters, Joseph bar Sabbas has the full roll-call of those who have been called to be disciples of our Lord Jesus. Besides the thirty-one here, there are some sixty more on his list, plus at least two secret disciples in Jerusalem.

"Going with our Lord will be the Twelve: myself, my brother Andrew, James and John the sons of Zebedee, Philip, Nathanael, Matthew, James son of Alpheus with his son Thaddeus, Thomas called the Twin, Simon called the Zealot, and Judas of Kerioth. My wife Concordia and Mary of Magdala will go with us also.

"Going to Bethsaida, beyond the reach of Herod Antipas, will be those men who were disciples of the Baptist: Daniel, Linus, Libni, and Shimei.

"Joseph son of Sabbas will return to Hebron, and in the spring he will bring back the disciples that are in the southern and eastern parts of Judea.

"Simon called the Leper will return to Bethany and bring back the disciples who are in and around Jerusalem.

"Mathias called Justus will return to Cana and bring back the disciples from western Galilee.

"Joses son of Alpheus will return to Ephraim and keep in contact with the Levites of Jerusalem.

"Susanna will return to Sennabris south of the Sea of Galilee, and Joanna wife of Chuza will return to Tiberias with her son Michael. These three will come back in the spring.

"Perez will return to Tiberias and maintain contact with Capernaum. The remainder will stay here in Capernaum: Beon and Bohan the fishermen; Gemariah and Tobias the teachers; and Matt son of Matthew who will watch over his family.

"In the spring, we will gather together in the wilderness southeast of Bethsaida to see what our Lord has for us then. See to it that you arrive there by the first day of Nissan.[17] Today our task is to collect the supplies for our journeys. Jesus will bid you Godspeed this evening."

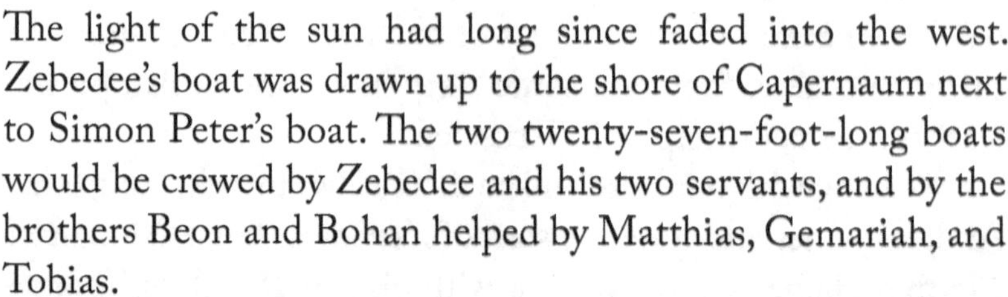

The light of the sun had long since faded into the west. Zebedee's boat was drawn up to the shore of Capernaum next to Simon Peter's boat. The two twenty-seven-foot-long boats would be crewed by Zebedee and his two servants, and by the brothers Beon and Bohan helped by Matthias, Gemariah, and Tobias.

Jesus had spoken with those left behind, and all fifteen passengers were gathered to depart, with their packs already loaded into the boats. Everything was ready.

John wasn't so sure about that. Here they were going off into the wilderness, maybe for miles, and they had only had a few hours to prepare. But Jesus climbed into one of the boats, and John followed him, along with all the others.[18]

7

ON THE BEACH

MONDAY, 24 JANUARY AD 29, 3:00 AM

Andrew helped Simon Peter beach their boat in the dark on the eastern shore of the Sea of Galilee. Zebedee and his boat were not far behind.

Andrew said, "Simon, our boat leaks like a sieve. I think I bailed enough water for every one of us to take a bath."

"Yeah, I noticed, Bro. That's because it's been pulled up on shore and hasn't been in the water for months. All the wood is shrinking. Not only that, but two of the oarlocks are coming loose, and it's getting harder to hold them together with just twine. We need to take this beast of ours up to Magdala for some major rebuilding."

"That's gonna take some serious shekels," said Andrew.

John helped Andrew and Concordia unload the packs of food, then watched as the two boats departed—Peter's boat headed to Capernaum, and Zebedee headed to Bethsaida.

John said, "Andrew, we've probly got enough food for all of us for maybe a week, but spring is more than two months away. I wonder how far we're going into this wilderness?"

"I dunno, John. I'm not going to worry about it. We've always had food to eat, even when we didn't know where it was coming from. But I think we have money to buy more."

John said, "Are you still carrying the money purse, Concordia?"

"No, I gave it back to the Keriothite. We're good on money. But I went over Judas' ledgers and it looks like there's quite a bit of money missing. I haven't reported this to Jesus. It seems like when I tell Jesus something, he already knows it."

Andrew said, "John and I suspected something like this before, but we didn't make any accusations either. We're just keeping our eyes open."

"Yes, I think that's the right thing to do," said Concordia.

John said, "Well, if we're going up onto the heights of Golan, I don't know of any market towns up there, just tiny villages. Maybe the money won't do us any good."

"You worry too much about food," said Concordia. "I'm more concerned about having decent clothes to wear."

<hr>

John and Andrew were bedding down beside Simon the Zealot and Thomas, as the eastern horizon began to hint at the approaching dawn. John said, "I hope we get on the road before all those people chasing Jesus find us. There's no end to the things they ask for, with healings and all."

Simon said, "There's more going on than you know, John. I saw at least twenty Zealots from Judea who came to see if Jesus was ready to lead an army against Herod and the Romans. They're furious over the death of the Baptist."

"Oh, wow, I didn't know about that," said John.

"Yes, and there were also two *Sicari* assassins in the crowd. They carry hidden knives to kill Roman sympathizers. I told

Peter and your brother James about them, but it's a death sentence to reveal the identity of a *Sicarius*."

Thomas said, "I'm glad Peter and James carry swords."

"No worries right now," said Andrew. "Good night, guys."

8

Not So Desolate

Friday, 28 January AD 29, 3:00 pm

John was right behind Jesus, who was striding ahead of his disciples toward the war-torn ruins of the city of Golan. Rocks were strewn about everywhere, and here and there were the remains of a wall or a dwelling. They had rested near the lake for a day before climbing into the Golan heights. At a leisurely pace they had covered some seventeen miles in the past three days.

Ahead John could see several houses that looked to be occupied. A man came out of the nearest house and saw them coming, and quickly ducked back inside. Just as quickly, he reappeared with two younger men and stood waiting for Jesus' band of men and women to get to him.

Jesus called out, "Hello, friend!"

The man replied, "Hello! Is that... Yes, it is! Jesus of Nazareth, you are welcome here! What a surprise!"

Jesus introduced each of his disciples by name, then said, "Children, this is Machir and his sons Jair and Nobah. They are among the few who still live here in Golan."

Machir said, "Welcome, friends! You are most welcome here. We are few, too few right now to even have a synagogue meeting. Here we grow figs and pomegranates, but the business caravans no longer pass by our front doors. They follow the new Roman road, five miles east of here."

Peter said, "It's a pleasure to meet you, Machir. We hope we won't be a burden to you. We've been looking for a refuge such as this, where we can rest and recuperate from our days on the road, going from town to town teaching."

Machir said, "I am also pleased to meet you, Simon Peter. And there is no burden so heavy that it could overbalance the teachings of your Master. Lord Jesus, will you bring us a Sabbath teaching tonight? Our ears are hungry for the truth."

Jesus said, "You are most gracious, Machir. Yes, I will teach this Sabbath, and also the next Sabbath. Then we will take our leave of your company and continue the journey that has been set for us by my Father in heaven."

"Oh, thank you, my Lord," he said. "We will be blessed to have you with us."

"Tell me, Machir, do you have scrolls of Scripture?"

"No, my Lord, only one. It is Book Four of the Psalms."

"That will do."

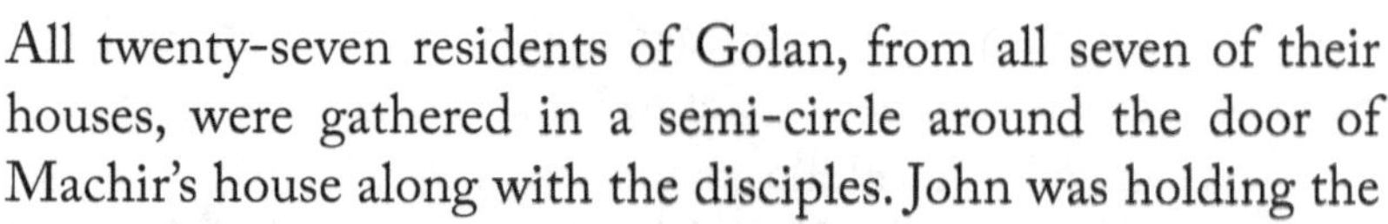

All twenty-seven residents of Golan, from all seven of their houses, were gathered in a semi-circle around the door of Machir's house along with the disciples. John was holding the scroll of Psalms, and gave it to Jesus as he stood up to read:

O Lord, how many are your works!
    In wisdom you made them all;
    The earth is full of your creatures.

There is the sea, vast and wide,
    in which are swarms without number,
    animals both small and great.

They all wait for you,
    to give them their food
    at the proper time.
You give to them, they gather it up;
    You open your hand, they are satisfied.
When you hide your face, they are dismayed;
    When you take away their breath,
    they return to the dust.
When you send forth your Spirit,
    they are created,
    and you renew the face of the earth.
May the glory of the Lord endure forever;
    May the Lord rejoice in all his works.[19]

Jesus gave the scroll to John, sat down, and began speaking: "Do you worry about what you will eat and what you will wear? I tell you, don't worry about your life, and what you will eat, nor about your body, and what clothes you will put on. For life is more than food, and the body more than clothing.

"Consider the ravens, who neither sow nor reap, and have no barn nor storeroom, yet God feeds them. How much more valuable are you than the birds! And which of you by worrying can add a single hour to his lifespan? If then you can't do this little thing, why worry about the rest?

"Consider the lilies, how they grow: they neither labor nor spin. I tell you that not even Solomon in all his splendor clothed himself like one of these. But if God so clothes the grass of the field, which is here today and thrown in the oven tomorrow, how much more will he clothe you? You men of doubt! You women of little faith!

"Do not set your heart on what you will eat and drink and wear, and do not keep on worrying. For the nations of the world eagerly seek these things, but your Father in heaven knows that you need them. Instead, eagerly seek his kingdom, and these things will be added to you.

"Do not be afraid, little children, for your Father has chosen gladly to give you the kingdom." [20]

9

· ·

HOME TO BETHSAIDA

John, Andrew, and Philip were walking north along the eastern lakeside path toward the boat docks below Bethsaida. John peered ahead saying, "I don't see my dad's boat at the shore. He must be out fishing."

Andrew said, "Look way off there to the south. I think that's Zebedee's boat out on the lake."

Philip said, "Yep, and there's my rowboat still on the shore ahead. Peter said he was gonna borrow it to take Concordia and the Magdalene back to his house in Capernaum."

"Hey look, there's someone coming from Capernaum on the western path," said John. "It looks like Matthias!"

"YO, MATTHIAS!" shouted Andrew. The figure in the distance stopped at the bottom of the road leading up to Bethsaida and waited for them.

When they got to the docks they exchanged greetings, and Matthias said, "You guys are back already? Where's everyone else?"

Philip said, "Jesus sent us into Bethsaida three at a time, so we wouldn't attract attention. He'll be along in the evening."[21]

Matthias said, "Andrew, congrats! When's the big day?"

"What big day?"

"Oh shoot. I guess I wasn't supposed to talk about it."

"Too late now," said Andrew. "What's going on?"

"My mom's been in negotiations with your mom," Said Matthias. "I guess they haven't included your dad Jason or my dad Lucius yet. Nothing can be whispered about this until both fathers come to an agreement."

Andrew was alarmed. "What! What are they up to?"

"Okay, I'll let you in on it. But you have to promise to keep quiet until your dad announces it. And the same thing for Philip and John. I'm just the mailman. Everything I know comes from my two sisters. I'll get in big trouble."

Philip said, "You better tell us now, or all three of us will toss you into the lake!"

Matthias laughed. "You can try. But here's the deal: Salome and my mom have been negotiating to set up a betrothal agreement between Andrew and my youngest sister Lilly. So, one year after that, you're going to be married!"

"What! This is the first I've heard of this," said Andrew.

John was excited. He said, "Lilly! Isn't that one of the two girls I saw you with when Jesus' sister Anna[22] had her wedding in Cana?"

Andrew said, "Yeah, the three of us were having a good conversation and a lot of fun."

Matthias said, "Yes, and Jesus' mom saw you having a good time, and she told your mom about it, and that's how it all got started."

John said, "Who was the other girl talking with them?"

Matthias said, "That was my other sister Rose. Our moms are working on a deal to betroth Rose to your brother James."

"What! He doesn't know anything about this!" said John.

"I know that now. But you guys have to keep quiet about this or I'll be in big trouble. I'm delivering a letter from my mom to Andrew's mom. Or maybe it's a proposal letter from my dad to your dad, Andrew. I don't really know what's in it."

"Well, I'm gonna tell James at least," said John. "This is too wild."

Matthias said, "John, be sure to tell your brother to keep quiet about this until your dad says something about it."

When the four disciples reached Zebedee's house, they found that Matthew, Thomas, and Big James had arrived before them. John saw that Matthew seemed ill at ease, as if he had something to say but was holding it back.

A big meal had been planned for this night. Apparently Jonas and his wife—the parents of Simon Peter and Andrew—had been invited over. James went out to get some extra wood for the kitchen fire. John saw his chance and followed him out. He briefed James on what was going on.

"What?" said James. "Rose is a fire-dragon, and I like her a lot, but I didn't know anything like this was happening. Dad must have saved enough money to build a house for me. Or to buy one. I sure don't have that kind of money."

"Yes, but you have to keep quiet until dad says something about this. If it comes out that this was happening behind his back, he'll lose honor in Bethsaida."

James sighed. "You're right, John. I guess you've learned some things about honor and shame from that time you stole dad's boat."

John was silent, as those scenes from two years ago flashed through his mind.

James was chopping wood and John was stacking it when their father arrived with his two servants Samuel and Sheva, along with the Bashan brothers Beon and Bohan, who had been helping him operate the fishing boat. Zebedee greeted his two sons, but like Matthew, he also seemed distant, as if he were holding something back. Zebedee helped James and John carry firewood into the house.

Then Peter arrived with Concordia and Mary Magdalene, saying, "We got here later than we wanted to. I'll take the women over to Capernaum in the morning."

"Oh, no," said Zebedee. "Let me take care of that for you. You can ride over and back with my crew."

The guests were gathering in Zebedee's small upper room, but some were missing. John couldn't see his dad, nor Andrew's dad. Matthias and Peter were also missing. The meal wouldn't start until the men arrived, and John was hungry.

John's mother Salome came through the door bringing in a small skin of wine and more cups. Wine! That meant that this was some sort of special occasion. John said, "Mom, where's Dad and the other men?"

"Oh, they went for a walk down by the beach. They'll be back soon, don't you worry."

Zebedee, Jonas, Matthew, and Matthias stood as wine was poured into each cup. But no one took a sip of wine yet.

"Welcome to my humble house, all of you," said Zebedee. "We have gathered to announce three upcoming betrothal vows of our sons and daughters. Jason and I are the fathers of the bridegrooms; Matthias is here to represent Lucius, the father of two of the young women; and Matthew is the father of the third."

John was shocked. Three women? What's going on here?

Zebedee continued. "The eldest is my son James. Lucius, the father of Rose, has given permission for his eldest daughter to be betrothed to James during this coming summer."

Jonas spoke next: "The next oldest is my son Andrew. Lucius has given permission for his youngest daughter Lilly to be betrothed to Andrew, also during this coming summer."

Zebedee spoke again: "The youngest is my son John, who will be entering into an intention with Sarah, daughter of Matthew."

John almost jumped up in shock, but he stifled himself.

Then Matthew spoke: "I have given permission for my daughter Sarah to express an intention to be betrothed to John next year, when she becomes fifteen years old."

Matthias said, "Let us all drink to the happiness and good fortune of all these who are intending betrothal!"

John was in the kitchen with Concordia and Mary the Magdalene, cleaning up after supper. They were talking about all the announcements that had been made at dinner.

John said, "But Sarah's only thirteen years old!"

Mary said, "In my clan, there are girls who are betrothed by their families when they're only twelve years old."

Concordia said, "We don't do that in the clans around here. More often the girl is fourteen or fifteen. I don't think there would be any disgrace or shame if you or Sarah wanted to back out before the betrothal. You're both very young."

Mary said, "It was different for me. I was thirteen, and my parents wanted to betroth me to a man who was thirty years older than me. He was very rich, and was paying a big bride-price. When I refused him, my family disowned me."

Concordia said, "I've heard of that happening. But John's dad and Sarah's dad would never do anything like that."

John was mollified a bit. He said, "I've gotta do a lot of thinking about this. Nobody's asked Jesus how he feels about it. I'm going to ask him for his advice."

10

COUNT THE COST

FRIDAY, 11 FEBRUARY AD 29, 4:00 AM

John felt that familiar touch on his shoulder and rolled out of his sleeping pallet. Jesus was going down the stairs, so John got up and followed him. Waiting outside were James and Andrew, which he didn't expect. Jesus, wearing his robe with the hood, motioned for them to follow him. They found a low hill out of town and the four of them prayed until dawn, with Jesus on the next hill over.

When the sun came up, Jesus joined the three young men. John asked, "When did you arrive, Teacher?"

"It was after dark when I got here with the Zealot and our man from Kerioth. Your mother Salome left some food out for us, which was nice. Peter was awake, and he told me about the surprises that came with your feast yesterday."

James said, "The more that I thought about it, the madder I got. How could they do this without telling us? But my dad told me that since we had been away for most of the year, there was no chance to bring us in on what was happening."

Andrew said, "Matthias said his two sisters approved of what was going on, which is encouraging. I guess they think this is a good thing."

John said, "I'm told that Sarah only found out about this a week ago. I hope she's not angry. But I'm worried about other things, Teacher."

"Tell me your worries, John."

"Well, we're your disciples, but none of us have asked your permission, or even your advice."

"Good thinking, John. There is much that my disciples will be doing. They will see distant lands and seldom be home. They and their wives need to sit down and carefully count the cost. This gospel of the kingdom must be preached as a testimony to all the nations, and then the kingdom of God will come." [23]

James said, "I think I'm going to be some kind of warrior for God, using words instead of swords. I think my wife would have to be a warrior also. Rose is kind of a warrior."

"Good thinking, James," said Jesus. "But there is more you do not yet know. You all will see a time of great trouble. Those with wives or children will bear a greater burden. Those who are nursing or pregnant will be in critical danger. And many of the massive works of mankind will be struck down."

Andrew said, "But, we are your disciples, Lord."

"Are you indeed my disciples? Who is first in your lives? If anyone comes to me and does not hate his own father and mother and wife and children, yes, and even his own life, he cannot be my disciple. He must be ready to carry his own cross and come after me." [24]

John said, "When will all this happen, Lord?"

"Only the Father knows the times and places for these things. By his will and according to his time they will happen. There will be a time to flee for your lives. But your own souls will be safe, and your Father in heaven is ready to welcome you into his arms. Ponder these things well, and count the cost, both you and your betrothed."

11

THE GATHERING

WEDNESDAY, 6 APRIL AD 29, 1:00 AM

"I see it! I see it!" Matt was excited.

"Where?" said John, peering into the dark.

"Over there, across the lake. I see the bonfire announcing the beginning of the year!" Philip, Nathanael, and Thaddeus also looked in the direction Matt was pointing.

"Oh, yeah, there it is," said Philip. "Quick! Let's light our fire so the watchers up at Gamla can see it."

"Matt and I have to be the first ones to light it 'cause we're the Levites," said Tad. They touched their torches to the tall pile of wood and branches they had built.

"Oh, right," said John. "Tell me again why they do this every year."

Nathanael said, "The Supreme Council meets to see if anyone has seen the new moon which begins the new month. If they did, they light a bonfire on the Mount of Olives so the next watchtower will know. Since we saw the bonfire across the lake, that means they saw the new moon, and yesterday was the first day of Nissan, the beginning of the new year."

John said, "So now there's more bonfires and watchmen all the way from here north to Damascus?"

"Yes," said Tad. "Oh, look! The bonfire in Gamla is lit!"

"That was fast," said Philip. "Where's the next one?"

"I don't know," said Matt. "But we're done. We can go back to Philip's house and go to bed."

"This was fun," said Nathanael. "But I'm not sleepy. There's been too much excitement going on in Bethsaida."

"I've been stuck in Capernaum and it's been boring with Jesus not there," said Matt. "What's been happening here?"

Nathanael said, "Word got out that Jesus called his ninety disciples to come here before the second Sabbath in Nissan. Simon the Zealot has been hearing a rumor speculating that Jesus is taking his disciples into the wilderness to get ready for an uprising against Herod and the Romans."

"I wouldn't put much faith in that rumor," said John.

"You're right," said Philip. "But that might explain why there's so many people gathering in Bethsaida and the other towns around us."

"People are even gathering up north in Gamla," said Matt.

"It's not just the Zealots who are gathering," said Nathanael. "Many more are coming just to be healed, or to hear Jesus teach. And others are thinking he's gonna do some great sign of power."

"Maybe that's what'll happen," said Philip. "It looks like Jesus will be in the wilderness with us during Passover, instead of on his way to Jerusalem.[25] Maybe he'll re-enact one of the signs that Moses did in the wilderness."

"I dunno about that, Philip," said John.

"Still, I expect this will be a big month," said Nathanael. "I'm looking forward to it."

12

FIVE THOUSAND FED

SUNDAY, 17 APRIL AD 29, 7:00 AM

Thaddeus and John arrived at Philip's house, panting and out of breath. They had just run all the way up to Bethsaida from the lake. John called out, "Simon! Jesus is calling us! He wants us all to get in the boat. Andrew and James are already there."

Simon Peter came out the door followed by the rest of the Twelve. He said, "Okay, we're ready to go. The others have already gone on foot to the meeting place."

Tad said, "Where's it gonna be?"

"It's a grassy valley in the heights about a mile up from the lake. The boat is ready for us; let's go!"

They were followed to the lake by dozens of visitors from the streets of Bethsaida, who had been shadowing the disciples. Hundreds more were already at the lake. With Jesus and the Twelve on board Peter's boat, they set sail and were pushed along the shoreline of the Sea of Galilee by a gentle breeze. But when the crowds from town saw them leaving, they began following them on foot along the shore.[26]

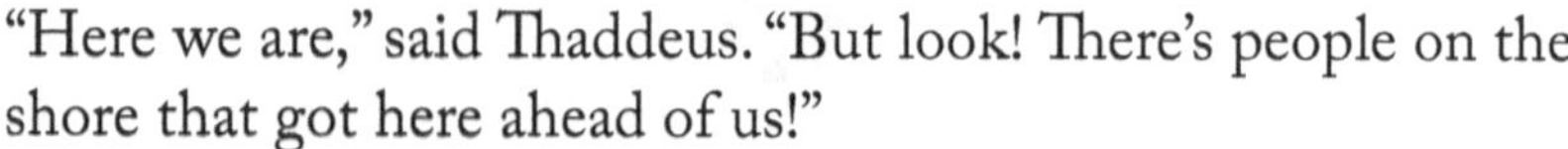

"Here we are," said Thaddeus. "But look! There's people on the shore that got here ahead of us!"

Philip and Andrew struck the sail while Peter and James jumped out of the boat and pulled it to shore. Jesus went ashore and welcomed the crowd, with John at his side.

Jesus said, "John, these are like sheep without a shepherd. They need to know the love of the Father for them." Some of them were sick, and Jesus began healing them.

Then he said, "Let's go up the mountain, for I have many things to teach."

Jesus and the Twelve climbed the Golan heights to where there was a valley with lots of grass. The rest of his disciples were there waiting for him. Jesus sat down on a high point, and spoke to them about the kingdom of God, while the crowd continued to gather, becoming larger every hour.[27]

John and Philip found Simon the former Zealot walking among the crowds with Judas of Kerioth. John said, "Simon, have you seen any Zealots here?"

"Yes, John," he replied. "There's at least two hundred of them. They're hoping that Jesus will proclaim a rebirth of the Kingdom of Israel and the removal of Herod and the Romans."

John was stunned. He said, "But… but it's pretty clear that's not going to happen, at least not today."

"You're right about that, John," said Simon. "I'm afraid they'll try something desperate, like seizing Jesus and declaring him to be the new king. I warned Peter and James and the Bashan brothers, and they're sticking close to Jesus with their hidden swords."

John said, "Oh wow. This is not good. What about the Sicarii? Have you seen any of them?"

"There's at least ten that I could see. Maybe more, considering that there's at least five thousand men here. I warned Matthew and Perez to be on their guard. Both of them used to work for Herod, and some crazy Sicarius might consider them justifiable targets for assassination."

"Oh, no. I hadn't thought of that," said John.

"We all need to stay alert," said Judas.

Philip said, "I've been thinking more about food. Today is one of the appointed fasting days, so the crowd isn't carrying food. Whatever snacks they did bring they've already eaten."

John said, "But the Passover Festival starts at sundown! Everyone will be thinking of food then!"

Judas said, "The only one that planned ahead was Amram, Matthew's son. He brought food for his sister and younger brothers."

Simon said, "The sun will be down in an hour. Let's get the Twelve together and go talk to Jesus about this."

———————•••●•••———————

Jesus had just healed a woman who had sprained her ankle, when the Twelve came to him. Philip said, "Teacher, this is a deserted place and the hour is late. We should send the crowd away to buy food for themselves in the villages round about."

Jesus said, "They need not go away. You give them something to eat. Philip, where would we buy bread so that these people may eat?"

Judas of Kerioth said, "We have only two hundred denarii in the purse."

Philip said, "Two hundred denarii wouldn't buy enough food for each person to get even a little piece."

Jesus said, "How many loaves do you have? Go and see."

Andrew said, "There's a boy here who has five small barley loaves and two fried fish. But what is that among so many people?"

"Bring them here to me, and have the people sit down."

Jesus let the people sit down on the grass in groups of fifties and hundreds, while Philip found Amram and brought the food to Jesus.

Taking the five loaves and the two fish, Jesus looked up to heaven and said, "Blessed are you Lord God, King of the universe, who brings forth bread from the earth."

Then he broke the loaves and gave them to the disciples, and the disciples gave them to the people. All the people ate and were satisfied.

Jesus called the Twelve together and said, "Gather up any leftovers, so that nothing is lost. Then I want you to leave immediately for Capernaum. I will come along after you when I finish praying." So they gathered up the food and filled twelve baskets with broken pieces of bread and fish, while Jesus began dismissing the crowd.

But some in the crowd began chanting, "This is the Prophet who is come into the world! This is the Prophet who is come into the world!" The chant spread through the crowd, repeating over and over.

Suddenly a group of some fifty men began rushing up the hill from which Jesus had been teaching. John was dismayed. He was on the far side of the little valley with Andrew, and felt helpless. He said, "Andrew! They're trying to capture Jesus to make him king!"

They both began running to help Jesus, but when they got there, he was nowhere in sight. The men that had rushed the hill were casting about in confusion, saying, "Where is he? Where did he go?"

Andrew said, "He slipped away, John."

Peter and James arrived, and Peter said, "Let's go down to the boat. Maybe Jesus is waiting for us there."

Simon and Judas arrived at the hilltop. Simon said, "The Zealots have sprung their trap, but they came up empty. They're gonna need a better plan than this to trap Jesus."

The rest of the Twelve arrived and began walking down to the boat, leaving the baskets of leftovers for the other disciples to give to the poor in Bethsaida.

The sun had long since set, but Jesus was nowhere in sight at the shoreline of the lake.

John said, "He's probly on a mountaintop praying."

Philip said, "Should we wait for him?"

Peter said, "No, Jesus told us to leave immediately for the other side, and that he would be along later. Let's start; the wind is blowing our direction."

Nathanael said, "We need to hurry. Those clouds in the west mean there's a storm coming."

The twelve got in the boat and pushed off, while John and Andrew set the sail. A puffy wind from the east took them away from the shore, and then stopped.

Abruptly, a violent gust of wind hit them from the west and a loud "CRRRACKKKK" came from the boat. Peter said, "The main mast is broken! Quick! Take down the sail!"

John and Andrew scrambled to take it down and almost lost it overboard as a stiff wind hit them from the west. The sky clouded over, it started raining, and the disciples began rowing in the dark against the wind.[28]

And John had just seen his sixteenth Passover.

13

WALKS ON WATER

MONDAY, 18 APRIL AD 29, 4:00 AM

Night had come upon the disciples in the boat. They were making slow headway, struggling to row against a stiff wind. The sea was rough, and waves were beating against the boat.

John and Andrew were taking a turn at the oars along with Simon the Zealot and Judas of Kerioth. Big James was at the tiller in the stern, and Peter was in the prow of the boat.

Peter was peering into the east behind them. He said, "I can't see the shoreline any more. We must have made three or four miles so far."

Philip said, "We're already in the fourth watch of the night. We'll be seeing daylight in the east soon."

Peter exclaimed, "Woah! What's that behind us?"

Thaddeus said, "It's a ghost!"

John peered into the darkness and saw what looked like a man. He said, "It's walking on the water! It's coming closer!"

Thomas said, "Is that my Lord Jesus?"

It was indeed Jesus, walking on the water. He said, "Take courage, friends! It's me! Don't be afraid."

Peter said, "Lord, if it's you, command me to come to you on the water."

Jesus said, "Come!"

Peter got out of the boat and began walking on the water toward Jesus. Then a gust of wind struck him, and he looked up at the storm clouds and began to sink.

Peter cried out, "Lord, save me!"

Jesus reached out his hand and took hold of Peter. He grinned at him and said, "O man of little faith, why did you doubt?"

Jesus and Peter got into the boat, and immediately the wind stopped.

Thomas said, "It's good to have you with us, Master. Truly you are the holy one of God."

John fell silent. He thought, "*Who is this guy? I thought I knew him.*" He pondered over the five loaves that were enough to feed five thousand, and Jesus walking on water, but he didn't understand any of it.

James looked ahead from his position at the stern, and said, "Hey, there's the shore! We're here already!" [29]

When they reached land, they found several wooden posts along the shoreline where they moored the boat among others tied there. The disciples disembarked, and Thaddeus looked around, saying, "Where are we, anyway? I thought we were going to Capernaum."

John said, "This is the shore of Gennesaret. Capernaum is away to the north. That wind blew us way off course. More south than this and we'd be in Magdala."

Two men a little way down the beach were running toward them. When they got close, one of them asked, "Hey, isn't that Jesus, the healer we've been hearing about?"

John said, "You're right, sir. We just got here."

The man said to Jesus, "Lord, come stay with us tonight, and all those with you. My aunt is sick, and she has been praying to meet you so she may be healed."

Jesus agreed, and the two men ran ahead of them to the village in the distance.

14

GENNESARET

MONDAY, 18 APRIL AD 29, 10:00 AM

When the people of Gennesaret heard that Jesus was sitting down in their marketplace, they sent men running to the neighboring villages, saying, "The healer is here!"

The men of the surrounding countryside began bringing those who were sick and laying them on their pallets before Jesus in the marketplace.

The sick begged Jesus that they might just touch even the fringe of his cloak, and they would be healed. Those who touched his clothes were made well.[30]

In the afternoon, John and most of the Twelve were relaxing in the marketplace, talking with the villagers about how more than five thousand were fed from only five loaves. Then to John's surprise, Joseph *bar* Sabbas and Matthias, Nathanael's cousin, showed up.

Nathanael said, "Cousin! We weren't expecting to see you so soon!"

Matthias said, "Yeah, we got a ride to Capernaum in a boat that was headed to Tiberias. They were charging one denarius per passenger—that's high seas piracy! Then we heard that Jesus was in Gennesaret. And it seems everyone in Capernaum knows you guys are here."

Simon the Zealot said, "Joseph, how are the rest of the disciples doing?"

Joseph said, "Most of them are still walking around the lake, and the crowds are following them. We might have eighty new disciples to add to the roll call. And I have some good news from that project you started, once we're in private."

Simon said, "Oh, come down this little alley and tell us now! I'm eager to hear."

Simon led the way into the alley, followed by Joseph, John, Andrew, and Nathanael. Nathanael was the first to speak: "So what's this secret project you've got going?"

Simon said, "Well, as you guys know, there were hundreds of Zealots among the five thousand across the lake. There was also a dozen of my friends from Hebron. We were trying to plant one or two of them as spies in the councils that the Zealots were holding."

"Yes, and that's our good news," said Joseph. "Both of your friends have been accepted into the inner council of the Zealots. They won't be able to surprise us with a fifty-man rush to grab Jesus again."

"Oh, that's great," said Nathanael.

"Not only that, but we found out that they had planted watchmen in high places above the shoreline, hoping they could kidnap Jesus if he tried to leave in Peter's boat. How *did* Jesus leave, anyway?"

John said, "If we told you, you wouldn't believe it. We should let Simon Peter tell that story. He had a special part to play in it."

"Oh, a mystery!" said Joseph. "I can't wait to hear."

15

. . . .

THE SEAL OF GOD

Jesus and the Twelve were walking north to Capernaum when they encountered a couple dozen people walking toward them. John recognized a few of their faces: some of them were the men who had run up the hill trying to capture Jesus.

He saw that Peter and James were tensely fingering the swords hidden under their clothes.

One of the men came to Jesus and said, "Rabbi, when did you come here?"

Jesus answered, "Truth, Truth I tell you: You are not seeking me because you saw marvelous signs, but because you ate your fill of bread. I tell you, don't go looking for the food that perishes, but for the food that lasts for eternal life. The Son of Man can give this to you, for on him God the Father has set his seal."

The man said, "God has set his seal on you? Then what sign will you do, so we may see it and believe in you? What work will you perform?"

Jesus said, "I tell you the truth, even if the earth had been covered in quail for you to eat along with the loaves, you would not have believed. But come to synagogue this week, and you will hear more." [31]

16

SARAH

THURSDAY, 21 APRIL AD 29, 9:00 AM

"Hey John, are you in there?"

John recognized Matt's voice at the gate of Simon Peter's house and went to open it. "Hi, Matt, what's up?"

"The singers for the Capernaum synagogue have gone to visit the synagogue in Magdala, so Jairus is gonna let me and Tad chant the psalm for the Sabbath morning service. Tad's dad is gonna teach us how to do it. Wanna come up to my house and listen to us practice? It'll be the first time I get a chance to do the duties of a Levite."

"Sure, sounds good," said John. "Hold on a sec; I'll tell Jesus that I'll be gone."

At Matt's house, what started out as a private lesson in the courtyard was turning into a public performance. Tad's uncle Joses was there to help with instruction. Also there to listen were Matt's mom and dad, his brother Amram, and his sister Sarah.

John was uncomfortable. Ever since hearing that Sarah was going to be promised to him as his future betrothed, he hadn't had a chance to talk with her to see how she felt about it. Not only that, but he still wasn't sure how he himself felt about it.

When the chanting lesson was over, the parents went back in the house, leaving the younger five in the courtyard. Sarah said, "That sounded good, you guys. I was kinda humming along with you when you were doing it. Wanna try it again with three of us singing?"

Together Tad and Matt said, "Sure," and the three of them chanted through the appointed verses twice.

John said, "Hey, I like that better with a girl's voice added. You sound good, Sarah!" Sarah blushed.

Amram said, "Sarah, you should sing along with them at the Sabbath service."

Matt said, "But only male members from the Levite tribe are supposed to chant the psalm. It'll cause trouble."

Tad said, "Well, I know that's the custom, but technically those rules only apply to the temple."

John said, "Do you think you could get away with it? That would be neat! I'd like to see it."

Tad said, "Well, Jesus is kinda taking over the service on Sabbath morning, and Jairus kinda said we could do what we wanna do. Plus, the rest of the rulers of the synagogue will be gone for some kind of special thing they're doing in Magdala."

Matt said, "Let's do it!"

Amram said, "Hooray! I'll go tell my brothers." Tad was excited too. He and Amram went into the house, leaving Matt, Sarah and John alone in the courtyard.

John stammered, "H– hey, Sarah."

"Hey, John," she replied.

"What– what do you think about our parents planning a betrothal for the two of us? Are they jumping the gun?"

Sarah spoke uncertainly: "Well, I know I'm only thirteen. But I'll be fourteen next month!"

She hesitated, and said, "I was more afraid that you might not like me."

John was taken aback. He said, "I like you a lot, Sarah. I guess I never told you. No, I'm just concerned with what Jesus is doing and what's gonna happen in the world. It might not be a good time to be starting a family."

Matt said, "I think it's our moms doing this. They probly think we should be planning grandchildren for them instead of following some prophet all around the country."

John said, "Yeah, you're right, Matt, at least as far as what my own mom thinks. What do you think about it?"

"I think you two are gonna have plenty of time to think about all this, and see what God might want us all to do."

Sarah said, "That sounds right, brother. I know I'm supposed to be turning into an adult right now, but I'd rather stay a kid for a little while."

John said, "Huh. That's what I feel sometimes too. A lot of the time I'd rather be ten years old."

Sarah laughed, then John started laughing. Soon Matt was laughing with them also.

Sarah said, "I'm glad I've got you two guys around me. We're going to be all right." She kissed her brother on the cheek, and then John on his cheek.

John was embarrassed. He had never been kissed before.

17

· ·

BREAD OF LIFE

SATURDAY, 23 APRIL AD 29, 9:00 AM

The synagogue service in Capernaum was under way. Jairus was seated at the front, with James son of Alpheus standing behind him. Jesus was seated near Jairus, with John standing behind him.

Jesus' disciples had made their way into the synagogue, and there was standing room only. The three young Pharisees assigned to shadow Jesus—Terah, Talmon, and Temeni—had worked their way up front to be near him.

Thaddeus and Matt were standing near the front of the curtain that divided the men's and women's sections, from which all those present could see Jairus and Jesus in the front. Sarah was standing unnoticed near Matt, but still within the women's section.

Jairus stood up, and Little James handed him the scroll of Exodus, the second book of the law of Moses. Jairus held it up high and processed around the congregation, with James clearing a path in front of him and his brother Joses following behind. Returning to the front, Jairus opened the scroll, found his place, and began to read:

The Lord said to Moses, "Behold, I am about to rain bread from heaven for you, and the people shall go out each day to gather a day's portion. Say to the people, 'At twilight you shall eat meat, and in the morning, you will be filled with bread. Then you shall know that I am the Lord your God.'"

In the evening quail came and covered the camp, and in the morning dew lay around. When the dew dried, on the face of the wilderness there was a fine, flake-like thing, fine as frost on the ground.

Moses said to them, "This is the bread that the Lord has given you to eat. Gather it, each one of you." Some gathered more, and some less. Those who gathered more had nothing left over, and those who gathered less had no lack. Morning after morning they gathered, each as much as he could eat.[32]

Jairus gave the scroll back to James and sat down. Then Thaddeus and Matt began chanting the psalm, with Sarah joining in:

> The people spoke against God, saying,
>> "Can God spread a table in the wilderness?
>> Can he really give bread
>> or provide meat for his people?"
> When the Lord heard this, he was full of wrath;
>> a fire was kindled against Jacob;
>> God's anger rose against Israel,
>> for they did not believe in God,
>> and did not trust his saving power.
> Yet he commanded the skies above,
>> and opened the doors of heaven
>> and rained down on them bread to eat,
>> and gave them the grain of heaven.
> The people ate of the bread of angels;
>> he sent them food in abundance.
>> The people ate and were well fed,
>> for he gave them what they craved.[33]

At the end of their chant Jesus stood up from his chair, and John handed him the great scroll of Isaiah. Jesus found the appointed verse and began to speak:

Our Father in heaven says,
    "Come, everyone who thirsts,
    come to the waters;
And he who has no money,
    come, buy and eat!
    Come, buy wine and milk
    without money and without price.
Why do you spend your money
    for that which is not bread,
    and your labor
    for that which does not satisfy?
Listen carefully to me,
    and eat what is good,
    and delight yourselves in rich food.
Incline your ear, and come to me;
    Hear, that your soul may live;
    And I will make with you
    an everlasting covenant,
    my steadfast, sure love for David." [34]

Jesus gave the scroll back to John and sat down. He said, "I tell you the truth, these words have come to pass today in your hearing. Let the one who has ears to hear, hear indeed. Let the one who truly hears do the work that God has set out for him."

Terah the Pharisee said to him, "What must we do, to be doing the work of God?"

Jesus said, "The work of God is that you believe in the one whom he has sent."

Talmon said, "Then what sign will you do, that we may see and believe you? What work do you perform? Our fathers ate food in the wilderness, as it is written, 'He gave them bread from heaven to eat.'"

Jesus said to them, "In very truth I tell you, it was not Moses who gave you the bread from heaven, but my Father, who gives you the true bread from heaven. For the bread of God is he who comes down from heaven and gives life to the world."

Temeni said, "Sir, give us this bread always."

Jesus said, "I am the Bread of Life. Whoever comes to me shall not hunger, and whoever believes in me shall never thirst. I have come down from heaven, not to do my own will but the will of him who sent me. For this is my Father's will, that all who look on the Son and believe in him will have eternal life, and I will raise them up on the last day." [35]

A stir moved through the crowd, and John heard some grumbling. Jairus stood up to lead a final hymn and prayer, and dismissed the congregation.

John returned the scroll of Isaiah to the attendant, and somehow he and Matt and Tad made it through the crowd out the front door. There they found Andrew, Philip, and Nathanael.

Nathanael said, "Woah, Jesus really let'm have it today!"

John said, "Yeah, he's starting to reveal more about his true identity."

Three men from outside of Capernaum heard them talking and confronted them. One of them said, "Are you disciples of this Jesus?"

Andrew said, "Yes we are. Did you have questions?"

The man replied, "Yes. Isn't this man the Jesus *bar* Joseph, whose father and mother lived in Nazareth? How can he say, 'I have come down from heaven'?"

A knot of angry men was beginning to gather around them, angrily discussing among themselves. One of them said,

"How can this man give us his flesh to eat? What is he trying to say?"

Suddenly, Jesus was right in the midst of them. John was startled; he had not seen Jesus approaching.

Jesus said to them, "Don't grumble among yourselves. No one can come to me unless the Father who sent me draws him. As it is written, 'They will all be taught by God.' As the living Father sent me, whoever feeds on me will also live because of me. Whoever feeds on my flesh and drinks my blood will live in me, and I will live in them. I am the Bread of Life." [36]

Still more men overheard the discussion, and the knot of men grew larger. But Jesus had slipped away. This time John had spotted him leaving and followed him, almost grabbing onto his cloak to keep from being separated.

As they walked the back alleyways in Capernaum, John said, "Teacher, some of those men were really upset today."

"Yes, my child, and yet there were others—a few—that heard the word and planted it in their hearts to grow and bear fruit. The Father knows who he has called and who will listen. Don't be disturbed by these men."

"Thanks, teacher."

18

• •

DISAPPEARING DISCIPLES

John knocked on the gate at Matt's house and Sarah let him in. She was in the courtyard with her three youngest brothers: Izhar, now ten years old; Hebron, eight; and Uzziel, six.

"Hi, Sarah," John said. "How're you doing?"

"Just fine," said Sarah. "I heard you and Matt got caught in the middle of a circle of angry men."

"Oh, it wasn't that bad. Besides, Jesus came and rescued us. How did the psalm chant go? Did anyone complain?"

"My mom said some of the women were horrified that tradition was being broken. But most of them were delighted to hear a girl's voice in the chant. I don't know what the men thought about it."

"I think for the men, Jesus raised so much fuss over what he said after the *haftarah* that they forgot about everything else. But Jesus said that you sounded great."

Sarah smiled broadly.

John said, "Where's Matt?"

"He and Amram are with my dad and my two uncles. I don't know what they're working on. It might be about the disciples who don't want to follow Jesus anymore."

"What! I haven't heard this! What's going on?"

"They say that four disciples quit—out of the fifteen who walked with Jesus when he sent out the Twelve. And then at least a dozen more also quit, from the disciples Jesus called in from their homes. Plus, a bunch of new converts from the feeding of the five thousand dropped out of training. Simon the Zealot and Joseph *bar* Sabbas are trying to put together a headcount to report to Jesus. But I don't know any names."

"This is awful! What are we gonna do?"

"They're planning to meet with Jesus in the noon hour."

John was in Simon Peter's courtyard when Matt and Tad arrived, closely followed by Joseph *bar* Sabbas and Joses *bar* Alpheus. He opened the gate and said, "Sarah told me what's going on. This is awful! Why are people leaving Jesus?"

Matt said, "Well, it's what Jesus was teaching yesterday about eating his flesh and drinking his blood. Even some disciples who promise they'll never leave told me, 'This is a tough saying; who can understand it?'"

Joseph said, "I have the final count for now. Is everybody here?"

John said, "That depends on who's left. How many remain of the twenty-seven?"

"The Twelve are all with us, plus myself, Matthias, Joses, Matt, and Perez. The Four women and Joanna's son Michael are with us, but won't be here for this meeting. In fact, not a single female disciple on the whole list is leaving us."

John said, "That means…"

"That means that we lost Gemariah, Tobias, Beon, and Bohan, plus twenty from the roll call. But we still have forty new disciples from the feeding of the five thousand who remain."

Those last two names hit John like a body blow. Beon and Bohan had been employees of Simon Peter's fishing crew for years, and John considered them his friends. He said, "Well then, we're all here. Let's go upstairs."

Jesus surveyed the disciples seated around the room. He said, "I know some of you are grumbling about my teaching yesterday. Are you taking offense at this? What if you were to see the Son of Man ascending to where he was before?"

The disciples were silent.

"It is the Spirit who gives life," Jesus continued, "the flesh is no help at all. The words that I spoke to you are spirit and life. But some of you here do not believe. This is why I said that no one can come to me unless it is granted to him by the Father."

Simon the Zealot said, "We have lost twenty-one from the roll call, plus Beon, Bohan, Gemariah, and Tobias. We also lost thirty of the new disciples from the feeding of the loaves and fishes."

Jesus said, "And what of you, the Twelve? Do you want to go away as well?"

Peter said, "Lord, to whom could we go? You have the words of eternal life. We believe that you are the holy one of God."

"Did I not choose you, the Twelve? Yet one of you is a devil." [37]

John was shocked at that. But no one said a word.

19

TIRED IN TYRE

THURSDAY, 12 MAY AD 29, 2:00 PM

John said, "I'm tired. But this ocean breeze feels good." John and the rest of the Twelve had been walking for three days, following Jesus from Capernaum to the Phoenician port of Tyre, where they planned to get some respite.

Jesus had spent two weeks in Capernaum teaching forty new disciples, gathering them each day at Matthew's in the large upper room. But whenever Jesus or one of the Twelve left the confines of Matthew's or Peter's courtyards a crowd would follow them, asking for favors and trying to touch their garments. After the training of the forty, Simon the Zealot recorded their names and villages in the roll call, and Jesus released them to return to their homes and families.

Now they were nearing the city gates of Tyre. But several dozen people were there waiting for them by the gate. Peter said, "How did those people know we were coming?"

Andrew said, "I have no idea. We didn't even know ourselves where Jesus was taking us when we left town. And I haven't seen our three tag-along Pharisees for weeks."

Nathanael said, "Some people were watching us when we passed through the city of Gischala. A horseback traveler must have brought the news here ahead of us."

As they stepped through the city gate, a woman came forward and knelt before Jesus, saying, "Have mercy on me, Son of David! My daughter is greatly oppressed by a demon."

But Jesus didn't answer a word, as he led the Twelve into the house of the Jewish family where they would be staying.

⸻ •◦●◦• ⸻

John, Andrew, Philip, Thaddeus, and Nathanael were returning from the shoreline of the Great Sea, where they had been watching the waves and the passing of the great sea-going ships. But the same woman found them and followed them around, crying out, "Have mercy on me! Have mercy on me!"

Inside the house, they found Jesus resting. John said, "Teacher, that Phoenician woman has been begging us to let her in to see you about her daughter."

Jesus answered, "I have been sent only to the lost sheep of the house of Israel."

"But teacher," said Philip, "send her away. She keeps calling after us."

Jesus got up, and the six of them went out the door, where they found the woman still waiting. She fell at Jesus' feet, saying, "Have mercy on me O Lord, Son of David! Come and cast the demon out of my daughter, for she suffers greatly."

Jesus said, "It is not right to take the children's bread and throw it to the dogs. The children of Israel must be fed first."

She said, "Yes, my Lord. But even the puppies eat the children's crumbs that fall from the master's table."

Jesus was surprised. "O woman, great is your faith! For this statement, you may go your way. Be it done for you as you have asked; the demon has left your daughter." [38]

20

· ·

ARREST WARRANT

THURSDAY, 19 MAY AD 29, 2:00 PM

John was just beginning to feel relaxed when a knock came on the gate. Jesus and the Twelve had arrived at coastal Sidon this morning, and were staying at the home of one of the newest disciples. Then Jesus had gone with Matthew and his brother "Little" James to inquire at the local synagogue, while Philip and Judas Thaddeus went sightseeing.

John followed the small boy who was sent to open the gate, and was surprised by who they found there. "Elnathan! Clopas! You guys are a long way from home!"

"That's for sure, John," said Elnathan. "But Nicodemus sent us to warn Jesus about what's going on in Jerusalem."

"Oh, wow. Well, come on in! Jesus isn't here right now, but our security team is here: Simon Peter, my brother James, Nathanael, and Simon the Zealot. You can tell them right now if you want, and there's plenty room for you to spend a couple nights. I think Jesus is going to read the *haftarah* in synagogue tomorrow."

The "security team" gathered in the upper room to hear the report from Jerusalem, along with John, Andrew, Thomas, and Judas of Kerioth. Peter said, "You fellows have come a long way. How did you find us?"

"Yes, that's part of the report," said Clopas. "When we heard you were here we came by way of the Via Maris road along the coast. You know those three Pharisees who used to follow you around?"

"Yeah," said James. "What happened to them?"

Clopas said, "Well, they were originally hired by Caiaphas the high priest to follow Jesus and report on what he said and did and where he went. But Nicodemus talked to their rabbi, a Pharisee who's a member of the Supreme Council, and convinced him to call the three men back in. Their spying job was never authorized by the council, and their project was more an effort by the Sadducees for their own purposes."

Nathanael said, "Well, even without those three spies, people don't seem to have any trouble locating us. How are they doing that now?"

Clopas said, "Most cities have a few residents sympathetic to the Sadducees, and the high priest has been relying more on them to keep tabs on Jesus. Nicodemus heard that you guys were headed to Tyre and Sidon when the council got a report from a Sadducee in Gischala."

"I suspected that," said Nathanael.

Peter said, "What about Herod Antipas? Is there any danger to the disciples who used to follow the Baptist, if they travel with us in Herod's Galilee territory?"

"No," said Elnathan. "The rumor about danger to them was complete bunk. Antipas would still like to see Jesus and talk with him, but he's not making any effort to seize him.

Which brings up another point: there's a movement among the Zealots to seize Jesus and forcibly make him king."

Simon the former Zealot said, "Yes, we ran into that. They sent fifty Zealots rushing up the hill to try to seize Jesus, but he slipped away. They were also keeping watch over Peter's boat, hoping to kidnap him when he got aboard. But I have good news: We've planted a couple of operatives in the inner council of the Zealots to report on their plans. We won't be getting any more surprises like that."

Peter said, "But what are the high priests up to? Last year they sent ten temple cops to arrest Jesus in Gibeah, but we left town before they got there."

"Yes," said Elnathan. "That was another project dreamt up by Caiaphas. He got a lot of criticism for doing that without consulting the Supreme Council. The bad news is that now he does have the authorization to arrest Jesus. The Sadducees are solidly behind the idea, but to get things done they needed support from enough of the Pharisees.

"The Pharisees in the council are evenly divided, with one side wanting to throw Jesus in a pit or kill him, and the other side just wanting to hear him defend himself. A half dozen of the Pharisees actually sympathize with Jesus, but they won't reveal themselves unless it comes to a final vote. There's even two or three secret disciples of Jesus on the council, not counting Nicodemus.

"So, the Sadducees proposed that the Supreme Council issue a warrant to arrest Jesus. But that caused a big uproar, and the proposal wasn't accepted until they promised that it wouldn't take place on the temple grounds, and wouldn't happen amid crowds that might start a riot. They can only arrest him if they locate him with a minimum of his supporters around him."

"That's not good," said James.

"It gets worse," said Elnathan. "The next time they go out to arrest Jesus, they'll have more than a dozen temple cops, plus all of Caiaphas' personal security detail, plus a batch of rent-a-cops borrowed from the Roman garrison. You can expect maybe thirty men armed with swords."

"Woah," said John. "I guess that's why Jesus didn't go to Jerusalem for Passover this year. He hasn't been going into Judea at all lately. I wonder how long that will last?" [39]

Thomas said, "It sounds like they're getting ready to kill any disciples who get in the way of their arrest warrant. We would probably die with Jesus."

"Yeah," said Andrew. "It sounds like the arresting party would just kill Jesus and get it over with."

"No," said Clopas. "They have strict instructions to bring him in alive. The Pharisees want to hear him defend himself against all the things the Sadducees are saying about him. And they're not really interested in the disciples. They just want Jesus. They believe that if they get rid of Jesus all his disciples will just fade away and disappear."

Andrew said, "With all the conditions they put against a public arrest, they're going to have a tough time finding us. When it's necessary, Jesus knows how to move around without being noticed."

"That's right," said Judas of Kerioth. "Unless they find a way to plant a spy right in the middle of us, he's going to be hard to find."

21

TEN TOWN TERRITORY

SUNDAY, 29 MAY AD 29, 10:00 AM

Jesus and the disciples were passing through Gamla, in Herod Philip's territory. Jesus had led them east from Sidon and was now striking south toward the eastern shore of the Sea of Galilee.

When the people in Gamla saw Jesus, they remembered him feeding the five thousand, and a large crowd began following him as he walked briskly south. Then some men from Gamla brought a man to him who was deaf and had a speech impediment.

John followed Jesus as he took the man aside privately. He saw Jesus put his fingers into the man's ears, and touch his tongue. Then he looked up to heaven, sighed, and called out, "Be opened!"

Right away the man could hear, and he was able to speak plainly. Jesus warned the man and his friends to tell no one about this.

But the more he warned them, the more eagerly they proclaimed it to the throng. The crowd began bringing the lame, the blind, the crippled, the mute, and many others, laying them at the feet of Jesus to be healed. And as they traveled, they attracted people from villages along the way, who followed behind them.

———— ·•❶•· ————

Jesus sent Peter, Andrew, Big James, and Philip to Bethsaida to retrieve Peter's boat. Judas of Kerioth went along with them to buy food.

Then Jesus continued south alongside the Sea of Galilee, followed by a throng of people. When he reached the Roman territory of the Ten Towns, he went up on a mountain and sat down there.

John and Tad had stopped to talk with some children in the crowd and had fallen behind. When they caught up to Jesus they sat down around him with Nathanael, Thomas, Matthew and Big James.

Simon the Zealot was walking around in the crowd looking for familiar faces, and the five who had been sent for the boat had not yet returned. Jesus began teaching the disciples.

The crowd was astonished at the things Jesus had done, and at the authority of his teaching. They were saying, "He has done all things well! He even makes the deaf hear and the mute speak. The God of Abraham must be with him!" [40]

22

Four Thousand Fed

TUESDAY, 31 MAY AD 29, 5:00 PM

"We've about run out of food," said John.

Judas of Kerioth said, "Yeah, I didn't know we were going to stay here three days. I should have bought more."

Matthew said, "The crowd has been listening closely to what Jesus has been teaching, and they keep wanting to hear more. Listening carefully is a sure way to get Jesus' attention."

Nathanael said, "Yes, and there's not as much turmoil in the crowd, running this way and that."

Simon the Zealot said, "That's partly because the Zealot party hasn't come. There's only a couple dozen of them here. But I heard they still haven't given up on their idea to capture Jesus and make him king."

Thomas said, "Jesus is resting right now. Shall we bring him something to eat?"

John said, "No need. When he wants us, he'll call."

Jesus called the Twelve to him and said, "I'm deeply concerned for the people here. They have been with me for three days and have run out of things to eat. I don't want to send them away hungry, for some of them have come a long way and may become exhausted by their trip back home."

Thaddeus said, "Where can we get enough food to feed such crowds? This is really a desolate place."

Jesus said to them, "How many loaves do you have?"

Judas of Kerioth said, "Seven, and a few small fish."

"Bring them to me," said Jesus. Judas brought in the basket of food.

Jesus raised the basket and looked up to heaven, saying "Blessed are you, Lord God, King of the Universe, who brings forth bread from the earth!" Then he gave the food to the disciples, and the disciples gave it to the crowds.

All the people ate and were satisfied, and the disciples gathered up seven baskets full of leftover broken pieces. Those who ate were about four thousand men, besides the women and children.

Jesus dismissed the crowds, sending them away to their own cities. Then he and the Twelve went down to the sea, got into the boat, and shoved off from shore.

Peter said, "Where are we going, Master?"

"I must visit the village of Dalmanutha, behind Magdala. There are children of Abraham there who want to hear the good news of the kingdom of God." [41]

23

SIGNS AND SADDUCEES

WEDNESDAY, 1 JUNE AD 29, 3:00 PM

Jesus and the Twelve shared space overnight in four houses in Dalmanutha. In the morning, Jesus sat down on the steps of the house where he had slept. There he taught the people of the village, about fifty of them. He began with the message first brought by John the Baptist: "The kingdom of heaven is at hand! Repent and believe the good news!"

As Jesus taught, John noticed that several Sadducees and Pharisees had arrived and were standing around the edge of the village people. John was startled when he recognized five of them: they were the rich Sadducees and Pharisees who had come to John the Baptist at the Jordan River. The Baptist had denounced them angrily.

As Jesus prepared to leave, the two Sadducees came to argue with him. One said, "How can you teach these people, if you haven't been to a school and you're not a prophet?"

Jesus replied, "Ah, but you know nothing of the true school and the true prophet. If you did you would be repenting in sackcloth and ashes, instead of wearing rich finery."

The other Sadducee said, "If you are indeed a prophet, show us a sign that will confirm your claim."

Jesus sighed deeply. He said, "Why does this generation seek a sign? In the evening you say, 'We will have fair weather, for the sky is red.' Then in the morning you say, 'It will be stormy today, for the sky is red and threatening.' How is it that you know how to interpret the appearance of the sky, but you can't interpret the signs of the times?

"This is an evil and adulterous generation that asks for a sign. Truly I say to you, no sign shall be given to it except the sign of Jonah." Then he left them, went down to the lake, and got into the boat with the disciples.

Peter said, "Which way should we go, Master?"

"Take us to the other side," he answered. [42]

Jesus laid down to rest in the front of the boat, first saying, "Beware of the leaven of the Pharisees and the Sadducees!"

When they were under way, John was with the others at the back of the boat. John quietly asked, "What did he mean, 'beware of the leaven'?"

Thaddeus said, "Is it because we forgot to buy bread?"

Simon the Zealot said, "No, it must be because of this loaf someone gave us in Magdala."

Jesus raised himself up in the bow. He said, "Oh you of little faith! Why are you discussing the fact that you have no bread? Don't you understand? Are your hearts so hardened? Do you have eyes that don't see, and ears that don't hear?

"Don't you remember? When I broke five loaves for five thousand, how many baskets of pieces did you take up?"

Matthew said, "Twelve."

"And when I broke the seven loaves for the four thousand, how many baskets of pieces did you take up?"

Thomas said, "Seven."

"So how is it you don't understand that I wasn't speaking of bread? Beware of the leaven of the Pharisees and Sadducees!" And John finally understood.[43]

24

BLIND IN BETHSAIDA

SUNDAY, 5 JUNE AD 29, 5:00 AM

John was sitting by the shore of the Sea of Galilee, watching the fishing boats out on the lake. For a half-hour now, he had been watching his dad's boat moving slowly toward shore, as the workers on board cast out nets in search of fish.

When they reached the shore, John's dad threw the bow rope to him, and he began pulling the boat in. He was joined by the Bashan brothers who jumped out of the boat to help. Zebedee's servants Samuel and Sheva jumped out also and pulled with a second rope, hauling the bow of the twenty-seven-foot boat securely onto the sand.

"Thanks, guys," said John.

Beon said, "Is Jesus still in town?"

John said, "Yes, but we're headed up towards Julias this afternoon."

Bohan said, "We've been thinking we were too hasty to leave Jesus, and wondering if he would take us back."

Beon said, "Yeah, but how can we eat his flesh, and drink his blood? That's a hard word."

John said, "Guys, that's just another one of Jesus' parables. You know how he teaches in parables. I don't understand it either, but sooner or later Jesus will find a way to show us what it means. And then we'll learn something deeper. Sometimes I think Jesus' whole life is a parable."

Bohan said, "We've been talking with Gemariah and Tobias, and I think they're wanting to come back also. But we feel so ashamed for deserting him."

John said, "Why don't the four of you come to Jesus together? Jesus is merciful. I even saw him show mercy to a Phoenician woman."

"That sounds good," said Beon. But today we need to carry all these fish up to Jason's house and get them onto his drying racks. Bohan and I are going to help split and clean the fish."

John said, "I think Philip is there with his dad. If you see him, tell him I'm going up to Julias with Jesus at noon. He might like to come along."

"Maybe," said Bohan. "But I think he's chopping wood for his dad's smokehouse today."

John headed up to Jonah's house, his boyhood home. He was looking for Thaddeus. When he arrived, Tad and Nate were there, along with Peter and Tad's dad "Little" James.

"Hey, Tad," John said, "Wanna go up to Julias with me and Jesus? We'll be back in time for dinner."

"Sure," said Tad.

"Hey you know what? I was just talking to Beon and Bohan. They want to come back to Jesus. And I think that Gemariah and Tobias are coming too. They're ashamed that they left. But they were confused about eating flesh and drinking blood."

Nathanael said, "Jesus will let them back in. He's always ready to forgive."

Tad said, "What confuses me is this thing about a 'sign.' Jesus fed five thousand men with twelve loaves and four thousand with seven loaves. Weren't they good enough signs? But the Sadducees keep asking for another sign."

Tad's dad said, "Son, they're asking for a special kind of sign. The law of Moses says that if a prophet tells a prophecy and it doesn't come true, then he's not a prophet." [44]

Nathanael said, "Right! So if they can get Jesus to make some kind of short-term 'sign' prophecy, they will gain power over Jesus by taking his prophecy to the Supreme Council where they can pass judgment over his words."

"Wow," said John. "I didn't know that. So that's why the Sadducees are so hung up on getting a sign. They think it will add to their power at the Supreme Council."

"That's correct," said Little James. "By putting down Jesus the Sadducees would gain way in the power struggles inside the council. And they would strengthen their claim that authority comes only from the law of Moses, and that books of prophets like Isaiah don't have authority."

John was about to step out the door to where Tad and Jesus were waiting, when his mother Salome called out. "John! Wait, I have something for you."

"Oh, what is it, mom?"

"It's this old cloak with a hood that belonged to your grandfather. I want you to have it."

"How come, mom?"

"You've been going out alone with Jesus a lot, and that's getting more dangerous all the time. There's folk that want to seize him and make him king, there's folk that want to get a reward for capturing a criminal, and there's folk that just plain want to kill him. This cloak will help you hide yourself when things are unsafe."

John held out the cloak and looked at it. "You know, you're right, mom. And I've seen Jesus wearing his hood when he doesn't want to be seen slipping in and out of Jerusalem. Thanks, Mom!"

As John stepped out the door, some people were bringing a mostly-blind man to Jesus. They said, "Just touch him and he'll be healed, master."

Jesus took the blind man by the hand, but he sent the men who had brought him away. Then he led him out onto the road, and spit on the man's eyes and laid hands on him. Then he said, "Do you see anything?"

The man looked around and said, "I see people, but they look like trees walking."

Then Jesus laid his hands on his eyes again, and he opened the man's eyes. The man said, "Oh, I can see! I see everything clearly!"

Jesus said to him, "Tell no one about this, and go home. Do not even enter the village, but go straight to your house. And know that your Father in heaven has granted you this healing because of your faith." [45]

—————— •••••• ——————

Jesus and John and some of Jesus' newest disciples stepped out of the small synagogue in Julias, where Jesus was teaching and strengthening his new disciples. He said, "John, it's time to go on the road again. When we get to Bethsaida, go to Jonah's house and tell Simon Peter to call in the Twelve and prepare to leave in two days."

John said, "Oh, good! Where are we going, teacher?"

"Through Philippi and Galilee, to strengthen the disciples the Father gave me while you Twelve were in Judea."

John said, "Great! I'm excited!"

25

Peter's Revelation

Wednesday, 8 June AD 29, 5:00 AM

It was the Festival of Weeks,[46] when Jews celebrate the giving of the Law through Moses. Jesus and the Twelve were on their way to the villages of Caesarea Philippi in the domain of Herod Philip, northeast of Capernaum.

Jesus was praying with the Twelve on a hilltop above a small Philippian village. He rose from his prayer and gathered his disciples around him. "Tell me," he said, "who do the crowds say that I am?"

John said, "Some people say that you're John the Baptist, risen from the dead."

Little James said, "Some are saying you're the prophet Elijah, who has returned as promised."

Matthew said, "Others are saying that you're Jeremiah, or one of the other prophets of old who has arisen."

Jesus said to them, "But who do you say that I am?"

Simon Peter replied, speaking in Greek: "Lord, you are the *Christos*, the Son of the living God."[47]

Jesus replied in Greek, saying, "Blessed are you, Simon son of Jonah! For flesh and blood has not revealed this to you, but my Father who is in heaven. I tell you, you are *Petros*, and on this *petra* I will build my called-out gathering. The gates of Death shall not prevail against it."[48]

Jesus continued, "I will give you the keys of the kingdom of heaven. Whatever you bind on earth shall have been bound in heaven, and whatever you loose on earth shall have been loosed in heaven.

"There will come a day when you all will shout this word from the treetops and whisper it in the alleyways. But today is not that day. I charge all of you to tell this to no one until I have sent you out into the world." [49]

John, Andrew, Philip, Nate, and Tad – the five teens among the Twelve – were bedding down at a small house in one of the villages near Caesarea Philippi. Jesus and the others were at another house nearby.

John said, "Andrew, remember the day we met Jesus and I asked you if you thought we had found the Messiah?"

Andrew said, "Yeah. I said that either we found the Messiah or we'd been wasting our time hanging around with the Baptist."

Nate said, "Yes, and then John told us how he saw Jesus turn a hundred gallons of water into fine wine."

Philip said, "That's when we knew we weren't wasting our time."

John said, "But now we've been with Jesus two years and three months, and this is the first time he's revealed to us that he's the Messiah."

Tad said, "I have a feeling that we haven't seen anything yet, compared with what Jesus has in store for us next."

26

PARABLE OF DEATH?

SATURDAY, 2 JULY AD 29, 10:00 AM

Jesus was leading the way down the hill after the synagogue meeting in Sakhnin, a village in central Galilee, with Peter at his right and John at his left. The rest of the Twelve were following.

John asked, "Teacher, today you were telling how the kingdom of God is coming, and showing how it's also present even today. What has to happen before the kingdom of God comes in its fullest?"

Jesus said, "Little one, before that day the Son of Man must to go to Jerusalem and suffer many things. He will be rejected by the elders, by the chief priests, and by the teachers of the Law, and be killed, and on the third day be raised."

Peter looked startled by this, and blurted out, "May God be merciful to you, Lord! May this never happen to you!"

Jesus stopped abruptly and turned toward Peter. Every eye of the Twelve watched to see what Jesus would say.

Sternly Jesus said, "Get yourself behind me, Satan! Simon, you are a hindrance to me. You are not setting your mind on the things of God, but rather on the things of man." [50]

That evening after dinner, John was upstairs with the Twelve at the house of Ben Aiah, a disciple and Levite. Jesus had gone out to pray alone on a hilltop.

Tad said, "What was that Jesus was saying about being killed? Is that another one of his parables?"

"I don't know, Tad," said Andrew.

"I thought he was speaking plainly," said John. "But I still don't understand what he meant."

Little James said, "I understand what Tad is asking. Is this supposed to really happen, or is it a deeper lesson for the twelve of us?"

Big James said, "It's confusing. Peter and I are carrying swords so that Jesus doesn't get killed, and he's saying that he'll be killed anyway."

Simon the Zealot said, "I don't know what it means either. But I'm still going to be vigilant about any danger to Jesus or the rest of us. Jesus has more or less allowed us to carry these swords."

"It sounded like a prophecy to me," said Nathanael.

Matthew said, "And to me also. I wrote it down in the journal I'm keeping for all of Jesus' sayings."

Peter said, "I feel like I let Jesus down in some way."

Thomas said, "I know what you mean, Peter. But maybe all of us are going to be killed."

"Don't be so gloomy, Thomas," said Philip.

Judas of Kerioth was silent.

27

SAVE YOUR SOUL

SATURDAY, 23 JULY AD 29, 11:00 AM

Jesus and John stepped down out of the synagogue of Shiqmona into the fresh sea breeze, just as they had done last December. Jesus had come to read the *haftarah*, and stayed to teach for two hours before the service ended.

The crowd was excited and animated, talking with each other about the lesson Jesus had taught. One man came up to Jesus and said, "Great teacher, what must we do now? Should we follow after you?"

Jesus stopped, and called to the crowd and the Twelve: "Come! Gather around me and hear!"

He waited until there was quiet, and said, "Are there those among you who would come after me? I tell you, if anyone would come after me, let him deny himself, and take up his cross daily, and follow me.

"Whoever would seek to save his life will lose it. But whoever loses his life for my sake and for the good news, will save it. What will it profit someone if they gain the whole world, but lose their soul? Or what can a person give in return for their soul?

"If anyone in this sinful generation is ashamed of the Son of Man and his words, so also will the Son of Man be ashamed of that person when he comes with his angels. At that time, he will repay each person according to what they have done.

"But I tell you the truth, there are some standing here who will not taste death until they see the Son of Man coming in his kingdom with power." [51]

John walked into the upper room where their Shiqmona host was preparing to serve them dinner. Andrew, Nate, Tad, and Thomas were there, engaged in a spirited conversation.

Thomas said, "See, I told you. We're going to die."

Nate said, "Don't be ridiculous. Everyone has to die sooner or later. The only question is when will it happen."

Tad said, "No, if the kingdom of God comes with power and we're worthy, we'll live forever."

Andrew said, "The kingdom of God has already come. Jesus is here and he brought God's power with him."

Nate said, "That's true, Andrew. But he hasn't yet brought the final judgment when God sorts out who will enter the kingdom and who won't."

John joined in: "The way I'm hearing Jesus, he's the one who will do the sorting out. And we're with him."

Thomas said, "You're right, John. I shouldn't be so gloomy. We need to stick with Jesus no matter what."

Just then Big James walked into the room. He said, "What's up, guys?"

Andrew said, "We've been talking about the power of Jesus and the kingdom of God."

John said, "Jesus says we're gonna go next to Elijah's mountain. That's where Elijah showed God's power against fifty priests of a false god."

James said, "Mount Carmel! I've always wanted to go up there! That mountain's twelve miles long. I can't wait. We'll see God's power up there!"

28

• •

Elijah's Mountain

This week John and the disciples had been following Jesus through the small villages east of Shiqmona. Nestled on the northeast slope of Mount Carmel they found a small town called Yokneam, and took lodging there for the Sabbath, after Jesus taught in their synagogue.

The next day Jesus took Peter and John and Big James on a climb to the top of the mountain ridge, where even the Great Sea could be seen in the distance. As the sun began to set, Jesus said, "Pray with me here, friends, for soon I must face the trials set out for me by my Father. Don't let the enemy distract you from your prayers."

Jesus went a few yards away, and John knelt to pray along with Peter and his brother James. Minutes passed, and then hours. John was heavy with sleep, and James had already nodded off. Peter was awake, but just barely. John's thoughts started to drift, as if he were floating away in his father's boat fishing, and he began to fade into dreamland…

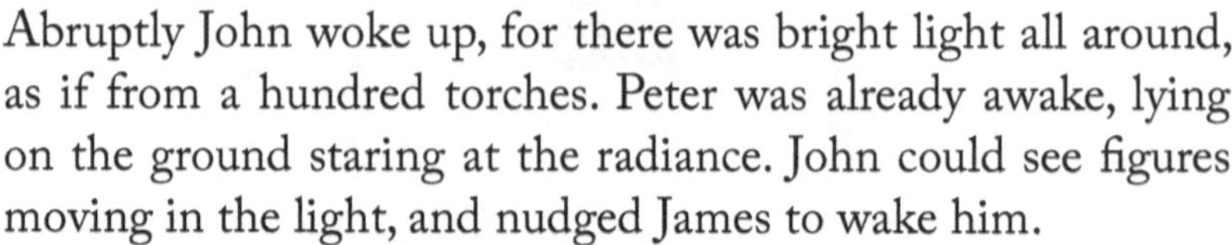

Abruptly John woke up, for there was bright light all around, as if from a hundred torches. Peter was already awake, lying on the ground staring at the radiance. John could see figures moving in the light, and nudged James to wake him.

The glare was blinding at first, but soon John could see that Jesus himself was the source of the light. His face was shining like the sun, and his clothes were radiant, dazzling white, as no cloth refiner on earth could make them.

Two men were standing with Jesus, speaking quietly in Hebrew. John thought he heard one of them mention an "exodus" like the time that Israel escaped from Egypt, while the other man said something about Jerusalem.

As it looked like the men were preparing to leave, Peter suddenly got up on his knees and spoke in a halting voice: "Great teacher, it is good that we're here. If you wish, I'll make three shelters here, one for you and one for Moses and one for Elijah."

Peter had barely spoken when a bright cloud came around them, and John was frightened as the cloud enveloped them. Then a voice came from the cloud, saying, "This is my beloved son, my chosen one. Listen to him only!"

When John heard this, he was even more terrified. All three disciples fell with their faces to the ground, afraid to look up. Then it grew quiet, and John felt a touch on his shoulder. It was Jesus, all alone. He said, "Rise, and have no fear."

Dawn was breaking, and Jesus began leading them down the mountain. He said, "My friends, I charge you to tell no one of this vision, not even the other disciples, until the Son of Man has risen from the dead."

James asked, "Lord, then why do the teachers of the Law say that first Elijah must come?"

Jesus said, "Elijah does indeed come, and he will restore all things. But I tell you that Elijah has already come, and they did to him whatever they pleased."

John thought, "*Oh, he must mean John the Baptist.*" But he kept silent, and told no one what he had seen.[52]

29

THIS KIND NEEDS PRAYER

MONDAY, 1 AUGUST AD 29, 8:00 AM

As Jesus, John, Peter, and James were entering the town, they heard a tumult of voices coming from the area of the synagogue. When they got closer, John could see that the other nine disciples were standing in the street with a crowd around them, and they were arguing with two teachers of the Law.

When the crowd spotted them, they ran up to greet Jesus, and were amazed at the bright whiteness of his clothing. Even his face seemed to shine. But Jesus came to where the disciples were standing, and asked, "What were you arguing about with them?"

Matthew started to say something, but right then someone from the crowd came up to Jesus and knelt before him, saying, "Lord, I came to bring my son to you, for he has an unclean spirit that makes him mute and deaf. I beg you to have mercy on him, for he is my only child.

"For the evil spirit will seize him, making him suddenly cry out. It convulses him so that he grinds his teeth and foams at the mouth. He becomes rigid and the spirit will hardly leave him. He suffers terribly."

Jesus asked the father, "How long has this been happening to him?"

The man said, "Since he was a toddler. When the spirit seizes him, it throws him down, and often casts him into fire or into water to destroy him. I brought him to your disciples and begged them to cast it out, but they were not able. But if you can do anything, have compassion on us and help us."

Jesus answered, "You say, 'If you can?' O faithless and twisted generation, how long am I to be with you? How long am I to bear with you? 'If you can!' All things are possible for the one who believes!"

Immediately the father cried out with tears, "O Master, I believe! Help me with my unbelief!"

Jesus said, "Bring your son here to me."

<hr>

As they waited, the two teachers of the Law withdrew to the edge of the crowd, watching to see what would happen. Then the father and his friends brought the boy to him. But when the boy looked up to Jesus, immediately he fell to the ground in convulsions, rolling about and foaming at the mouth.

As the crowd came running to see, Jesus rebuked the unclean spirit, saying, "You spirit of muteness and deafness, I command you, come out of the boy and never enter him again!"

The boy cried out and convulsed terribly, then went limp like a corpse. Many in the crowd murmured, "He's dead."

But Jesus took him by the hand and lifted him up. The boy arose, and Jesus gave him back to his father, completely healed. The crowd was astonished at the power of God.

As the disciples were entering the house where they were lodging, John asked Andrew, "So what was it that you guys were arguing about with the teachers of the Law?"

Andrew said, "They were accusing us of being a fraud, and deceiving the people with false healing power. We were saying that Jesus had all power, but they disputed that."

Jesus came into the room behind the last of the Twelve. Nathanael said, "Teacher, why couldn't we cast out that unclean spirit?"

Jesus said, "It was because of your little faith. Truly I tell you, if you have faith like a grain of mustard seed, you will say to this mountain, 'Move from here over to there,' and it will move. Nothing will be impossible for you. But this kind hardly comes out except through prayer and fasting." [53]

John couldn't sleep. Everyone else was fast asleep except Peter, who was missing. John touched his brother James on the shoulder, and motioned for him to come outside with him.

As they stepped out the door, Simon Peter was nearby, pacing about.

"I couldn't sleep," said John. "I keep thinking about what happened on the mountain."

"Neither could I," said Peter. "We heard the very voice of God talking to us up there, and we didn't die."

James said, "Simon, how did you know that the men talking with Jesus were Moses and Elijah?"

Peter said, "I really didn't know what I was saying. I just opened my mouth and words came out. One of the men was wearing a leather girdle like Elijah the Tishbite.[54] And the other one was talking about an exodus that Jesus would do. But really, all I was doing was babbling."

30

DEATH TALE RETOLD

FRIDAY, 5 AUGUST AD 29, 9:00 PM

Nazareth was quiet. The Twelve were in high spirits, for they were still marveling at everything that Jesus was doing.

Jesus was leading them in the dark along a private path to the back door of the house where he was raised. When they left Yokneam Jesus had said, "I have a teaching for you to consider well, and I don't want anyone to know where we are or what I'm teaching."

Jesus opened the back door and stepped in, followed by the Twelve. He said, "Ah, as I thought. My brother James is away at Jerusalem. We won't be disturbed here. And I'm sure there's plenty of food for us. Judas, take an inventory of everything we eat while we are here, and leave behind a double payment for my brother."

John said, "It's going to be cozy, for the thirteen of us."

Jesus said, "When I was living here with my parents and four brothers and three sisters, it never seemed crowded for the ten of us. But yes, it will be cozy.

"Peter, you and Big James and I will sleep in my parent's room, that my brother James uses. John, Andrew, Tad, Nate, Philip, and Thomas, you young people will sleep in the boys' room where I used to sleep. Matthew, Little James, Simon, and Jude, you older ones will sleep in the girls' room where my sisters used to sleep.

"Don't light any torches, for no one in town should know we are here. I'll serve tonight's meal, for I know where the food is stored. After supper, I'll have a short teaching for you. Tomorrow we stay inside for the entire Sabbath, relaxing and sharing and learning. We leave tomorrow after dark. Now go find your places while I go find the food."

The Twelve finished their evening meal, and crowded into the kitchen for Jesus' short teaching. Nathanael said, "Master, for working in the dark, you sure put together a great supper!"

"Thank you, Nate. But now settle yourselves. Listen closely, and let these words sink into your ears." Jesus continued with sudden intensity:

"*The Son of Man is about to be delivered into the hands of men, and they will kill him. And after he is killed, he will be raised on the third day.*" [55]

There was an uncomfortable rustling among the Twelve, as they tried to take this in.

Jesus continued, "This is the second time I have given you this teaching. Hold it well, and do not share it with the other disciples for now, nor with anyone else.

"Now find your rooms. The older men will serve the morning meal tomorrow, and the youngsters will serve the evening meal. Be of good cheer, for the will of our Father in heaven will be accomplished at its appointed time."

"Tad?"

"Yes, John?"

"Are you okay on the floor there?"

"Oh, yes, I'm fine."

"Sleeping in a bed feels like a luxury," John said. "I guess this is what you get when you have a house lived in by five kids who were carpenters."

"Yes, but John?"

"Yes, Tad?"

"What did Jesus mean when he said he would be killed, and then raised on the third day?"

"I don't know; I'm trying to figure that out myself."

Andrew said, "Do you think it's another parable?"

Philip said, "I don't know, but it's distressing. I'm afraid to ask Jesus about it."

Thomas said, "I'm with Philip: this is distressing."

Nate said, "His meaning seems to be concealed from us, as if we're not supposed to understand it."

John said, "The only thing that makes me feel better is knowing that Jesus has the power, and that he loves all of us."

Nate said, "Thanks, John. That's a good thought to go to sleep on."

31

WHO'S THE GREATEST?

TUESDAY, 15 AUGUST AD 29, 4:00 PM

"Daddy! Daddy! Daddy!"

Matthew braced himself as his three youngest children came racing down the road and bounded into his arms. "Izhar! Hebron! Uzziel! How are you doing? Have you been giving your mom any trouble?"

Uzziel, the youngest, said, "Oh, no, daddy! We been good!"

"Well, go tell mommy that Jesus is coming. There he is, way back behind us on the road."

Hebron said, "Mom's waiting for you at Peter's house!"

"Oh, boy!" said Izhar, "Jesus is coming! Let's go, guys."

The three of them went running off in the direction from which they came, shouting, "Jesus is coming! Jesus is coming! Jesus is coming!"

"Quite a welcome committee you've got there, Matthew," said Little James. "I'll say you'll probably get more of the same from the rest of your crew."

"That'd be fine, James, as long as all three of them don't try to jump into my arms at once. You'd have to peel me off the road."

James chuckled. "No, that wouldn't be decorous for the greatest elder of Jesus' disciples."

Matthew said, "I'm not the greatest! I may be the eldest of the Twelve, but Peter is the greatest one. He's the one Jesus uses to call us all together."

Peter said, "I don't know about this 'greatest' thing, but I was here before Matthew. Matthew was the last of the Twelve to join our road crew."

Nate said, "Well, Andrew was the first of us to meet Jesus, followed by John and Peter, who was with Concordia. Then there was Big James, and the next day was Philip and myself. I suppose that counts for something."

John said, "Don't forget that it was Tad who spotted Jesus first, raggedy sandals and all."

Simon the Zealot said, "Well, it's Judas who carries the moneybag. That makes him pretty important."

Tad said, "Jesus spends more time with John than any of the rest of us. When the kingdom comes, he should be the greatest."

John kept quiet as he listened to the Twelve bring up various reasons why one or another of them should be the most important one, as they began entering the outskirts of Capernaum.

•◦●◦•

There was a welcoming party waiting at Concordia's house. Paula was there with Amram and Matt. Sarah was standing behind Matt, and locked eyes with John across the room. John wished he could share with her what Jesus had been talking about. Sarah also looked as if she had something she wanted to talk about. But he just waved and said "Hi, Sarah," and she waved back, "Hi, John."

Mary of Magdala and Susanna of Sennebris were there, along with Joanna wife of Chuza and her son Michael, and of course Concordia's mom Perpetua with her servant Mina.

Nate's cousin Matthias was there, and Matthew's friend Perez. And to John's surprise, Daniel was there, his friend from the disciples of John the Baptist.

Jesus was last to enter the house, but he wasn't far behind the Twelve. He said to his disciples, "What was that you were discussing on the road?

"Oh, nothing important," said Peter.

But Big James said, "Teacher, which of us will be the greatest when the kingdom comes?"

Jesus said, "Ah, as I thought." Jesus sat down and said, "Listen, all twelve of you, and listen well." John and the rest immediately circled around him.

Jesus looked around. "Uzziel! Uzziel my child, come here." Jesus drew Uzziel next to him and wrapped his arm around him. Uzziel grinned happily.

Jesus said, "Truly I say to all of you, unless you turn and become like children, you will never enter the kingdom of God. Whoever receives one child such as this, receives me, and whoever receives me receives not me but the One who sent me."

And he said to them, "If any of you would be first, he must be last of all and servant of all. For he who is least among you is the one who is great. And whoever humbles himself like this little child of mine is the greatest in the kingdom of God." [56]

Somehow despite all the commotion in the room, with friends greeting friends and dainty food being served, John and Sarah were able to work their way over to a less crowded corner where they could sit. Paula glanced sharply at them from the kitchen, but then went about serving and talking.

Sarah's eyes flashed about the room, and she took John's hand. John felt stirred at her touch. He said, "What's going on, Sarah? You look troubled."

She said, "No, not troubled, just edgy with all that's going on. Did anyone tell you what's planned for this week?"

"No, no one tells me anything. I'm the last to know."

Sarah smiled. "Oh John, it's not that bad. They're not shunning you."

"I guess it's just that I'm almost the youngest. Only Tad is younger than me. But tell me, what's going on?"

"This is like only half the people in town for this event. There's another whole crowd at my house: Jesus' brothers and his sister Anna, Matthias' parents and sisters, Peter's and Philip's parents, and more."

"Uh oh. This must be about the betrothals of Andrew and my brother."

"You're right. It was supposed to happen last month, but you guys were on the road with Jesus. Now it's rescheduled for the first day of next week. But there's more."

"What else?"

"At the betrothals of Lilly and Rose they're going to announce the date of the betrothal between you and me."

John said wryly. "I love the way they keep me informed."

"Don't feel alone. I know they're going to do this, but I don't know the date they set. It might be the day I turn fifteen, right after Passover."

John squeezed Sarah's hand. "Well that'll be fine with me. I've had time to think about this and I really want it."

Sarah's face flushed, and she smiled.

John said, "But there's stuff you need to think about. Because I'm hanging so close to Jesus, there's real danger that I could be killed. Then you'd be left alone."

Sarah said, "I don't care, John, I still want this."

Now it was John's turn to have his face flush red.

32

BETROTHAL

MONDAY, 21 AUGUST AD 29, 8:00 AM

"Hey John, whatcha doing?"

John looked up to see his brother James, and said, "I'm picking my way through Jesus' scroll of the prophet Hosea. It's really interesting that Hosea's marriage was a prophecy of what God was planning to do."

James said, "I heard Hosea's story once in synagogue. It's fascinating."

John said, "I heard you say something to Jesus about you and Rose being warriors for God. Do you think your marriage will be some kind of prophecy or prophetic statement?"

"Wow, I'll have to think about that. But so far, you're the only prophet in our family."

"Huh. I don't feel like a prophet."

"Well, prophet or not, wanna come with me to meet dad at the docks? He's bringing stuff that needs to be carried up to Matthew's house for the feast."

"Sure, hold on while I put this scroll back in Jesus' room."

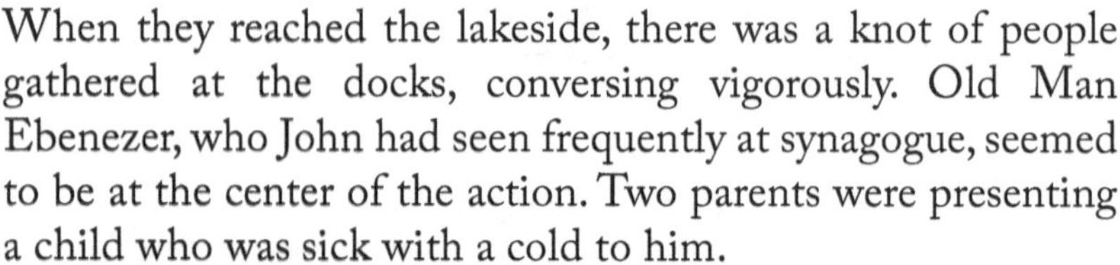

When they reached the lakeside, there was a knot of people gathered at the docks, conversing vigorously. Old Man Ebenezer, who John had seen frequently at synagogue, seemed to be at the center of the action. Two parents were presenting a child who was sick with a cold to him.

Ebenezer laid his hands on the child's head and said, "O you spirit of sneezing and coughing and sniffling, come out of this child and do not return, in the name of Jesus of Nazareth, the holy one of God!"

John was shocked. He had never seen Ebenezer travelling with any of the disciples, nor attending any of Jesus' discipleship classes. But apparently the child was cured, for he showed no more symptoms, and his parents were smiling and thanking the old man.

James said to him, "Old Man, how can you cast out spirits in Jesus' name when you have never followed him?"

Ebenezer leaned on his cane and said, "Perhaps the power of Jesus is greater than you imagined! As long as I am able, I will not stop helping people in Jesus' name." Then he laughed at them and hobbled away.

John opened his mouth. Then he closed his mouth. He could think of nothing to say.

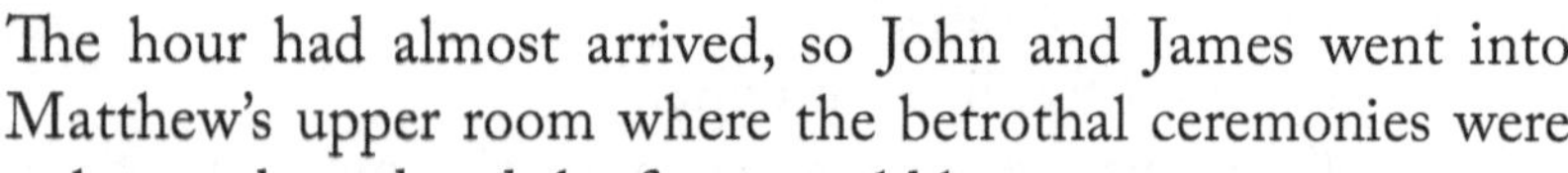

The hour had almost arrived, so John and James went into Matthew's upper room where the betrothal ceremonies were to be conducted and the feast would be eaten.

Jesus was already there, and John said to him, "Teacher, we saw someone casting out demons in your name and we tried to stop him, because he was not following us."

But Jesus said, "Oh, don't stop him, for no one who does a mighty work in my name will soon afterward be able to speak evil about me. The one who is not against us is for us. Truly I say to you, whoever gives you a cup of water to drink because you belong to me will by no means lose his reward." [57]

<hr>

"James, where's your future bride?"

"I don't know, John. I haven't seen Rose since we got back from Elijah's mountain. And Andrew hasn't seen Lilly either. We know they're staying here at Matthew's house, but they've been kept away in private. You're the only groom that's seen his future bride, and her mother didn't think that was such a good idea."

"Parents are weird. Where do they get these ideas?"

"Well, there's an ancient tradition that the bride isn't seen on her wedding day until it's time for the ceremony, so that she can dazzle everyone in all her dressed-up glory. But our wedding day is still a year from now, and yours is after that. You're right, parents are weird."

"Did you get a gift for her?"

"Yes, it's a bracelet with precious stones."

"I have a pendant with a silver chain for Sarah. Mom gave it to me. It was her mother's."

"Oh, look," said John. There was a flurry of activity at the door, and five men came in. First was Zebedee and Matthew, then Andrew's father Jonah, then Rose and Lilly's father Lucius, then Jairus from the synagogue, and then—surprise—Jaroel, the mayor of Capernaum.

But still no Rose, no Lilly, and no Sarah.

Zebedee, Lucius, Matthew, and Jaroel stood around a tall table in the middle of the room, where ink quills and sealing wax were laid out, along with cups filled with wine.

Matthew produced parchments with writing on them and said, "Behold, here are three copies of a contract for the intended marriage between James son of Zebedee and Rose daughter of Lucius, agreed upon by their fathers this day. It stipulates the payment by Lucius for the care of his daughter from the marriage day forward, and what will remain with her in case of the death of James. Zebedee and Lucius, sign here please."

They did so, and Matthew signed as witness to the contract. Then Jaroel said, "Behold, as mayor and notary of the city of Capernaum and by authority of His Majesty Herod Antipas, I set my seal on these documents and accept a copy into the annals of the city."

As John expected, Jaroel continued with a speech on how he was honored to be present, wished the families well, how this was a great day for Capernaum, etc., etc.

Then Rose came in a side door, radiantly dressed and escorted by her grandmother Myrtle. John remembered them from Anna's wedding. Jairus picked up the wine cup and said, "Let the future bride and the future groom drink from this common cup as a foretaste of their common life together."

Rose was blushing as she received her gift and drank a sip of wine with James. They stepped aside with their cup while Zebedee stepped back for Jonah to approach the table.

Matthew repeated what he had said previously, beginning with, "Behold, here is the contract for the intended marriage between Andrew son of Jonah and Lilly daughter of Lucius, agreed upon by their fathers this day." He and the two fathers signed the parchments, Jaroel set his seal on them and gave another speech, and Lilly came in radiantly, escorted by her mother Hazel. Jairus gave another blessing, Lilly received her gift, she and Andrew drank from their common cup, and they stepped back from the table.

"*Okay,*" thought John, "*What happens now? Where's Sarah?*"

But Matthew had more to say: "On this joyous occasion, we also are delighted to announce the intended betrothal of my daughter Sarah to John son of Zebedee. God willing, the contract will be presented on the first day of the month of Iyar, right after Passover next year. But today John and Sarah will also drink from a common cup, in anticipation of their future life together."

Sarah came in from the side door with Paula, and John was stunned. He had never seen Sarah in anything but simple children's clothes, but today she was dazzling. John placed the pendant over her head, and Sarah blushed.

Jairus presented them with their cup of wine. John took a drink, and gave the cup to Sarah. As she took a sip, John caught Jesus' eye over Sarah's shoulder. He was sitting against a wall, between his mother and the Magdalene.

It seemed to John that a look of deep sadness briefly washed over Jesus' face, just as their eyes connected. Then, just as quickly, Jesus regained his composure and turned to talk with Mary of Magdala.

And now the joyous feast would start.

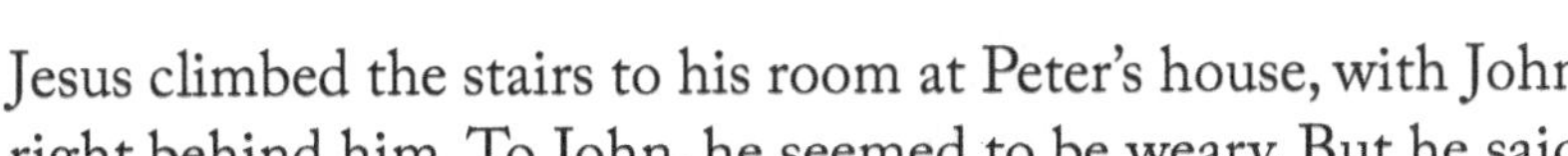

Jesus climbed the stairs to his room at Peter's house, with John right behind him. To John, he seemed to be weary. But he said nothing.

John settled down on his pallet in the corner of Jesus' room and said, "You seem tired, teacher."

Jesus said, "No, John, not tired. I'm just a bit melancholy."

"What's wrong, Jesus?"

"My time is coming soon. I have set my face toward Jerusalem, and I'll be leaving Galilee before long. This time I don't think I'll be coming back. It's a joy to have you with me, John. But don't worry about me. Just keep your heart set on the kingdom of our Father." [58]

33

CANA FEAST

TUESDAY, 30 AUGUST AD 29, 4:00 PM

John hurried to catch up with Andrew, who was way out in front of the rest of the disciples. He called, "Hey, Andy!"

Andrew looked back and said, "What's up?"

"What's the rush? What was that Matthias told you before he ran off? I didn't hear him."

"Well, you know we're invited to dinner by Anna's husband, don't you?"

"Yeah, looking forward to it."

"Well, the dinner isn't at Anna's place; it's at her father-in-law Maimon's, where the wedding was, and Lilly and Rose are gonna be there. Maimon is throwing a celebration for their betrothal, and it's about to start right now."

"Oh, wow, so you're going to be a special guest, then!"

"Well, sorta. Jesus is the guest of honor, and there's a huge guest list. Jesus' brothers and sisters are there, and some Pharisees and teachers of the Law from Jerusalem. They're friends of Nicodemus, Maimon's employer."

John said, "I thought Jesus' brothers were on their way back to Nazareth."

"They were, but then they got the invitation from Maimon, and they changed their destination."

"So, you're in a hurry to eat?"

"Silly boy. You didn't hear me. Lilly is gonna be there."

"Yeah, I'm just messing with you. I guess there's no chance Sarah will be there."

"Don't be so sure, John. Matthew is taking his whole family to the Festival of Booths at Jerusalem, and Cana is one of his stopovers on the way."

John felt suddenly uplifted. He said, "Well, what are you waiting for? Let's get going!"

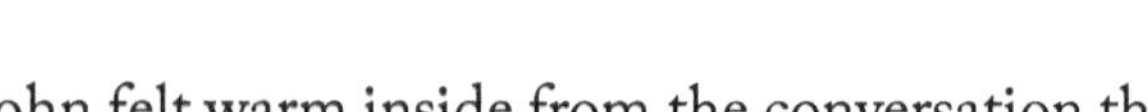

John felt warm inside from the conversation that he'd had with Sarah. But two Pharisees were approaching Jesus' table and they looked serious. "Greetings, teacher," said the one who appeared to be the eldest. Jesus greeted him in return.

"Teacher, we noticed that your disciples do not perform the hand-washing ritual before they eat, but eat with defiled hands. Why do they break the tradition of the elders like that?"

Jesus' face became stern. He raised himself up from his cushion and said, "And why is it that you break the commandment of God for the sake of your tradition? You are experts at doing these things!

"For God commanded, 'Honor your father and your mother,' and 'Whoever speaks evil of their father or mother must surely die.'[59]

"But you say that if a man tells his parents, 'Whatever you would have gained from me is given to God,' then you no longer permit him to do anything for his parents.

"You hold up your own tradition and make the word of God void! And many such things you do, such as the washing of cups and pots and dining couches. You hypocrites! Well did Isaiah say of you,

> This people honor me with their lips,
>> but their heart is far from me.
> Uselessly do they worship me,
>> teaching as doctrines the traditions of men." [60]

Jesus stood up and called to the guests, "Hear me, all of you, and understand! It is not what goes into the mouth that defiles a person, but what comes out of the mouth.

"Again I say, there is nothing outside a person that by going into him can defile him. It is the things that come out from a person that defile him."

* * *

John, Andrew, Peter, and James followed Jesus up the stairs to the room that had been set aside for them. Peter said, "Did you know the Pharisees were offended when they heard your saying about defiling?"

Jesus answered, "Every plant that was not planted by my Father in Heaven will be rooted up. Don't worry yourself about them; they are blind guides. And with the blind leading the blind, they will all fall into a pit."

But Peter said, "Teacher, explain this teaching to us."

Jesus said, "You don't understand? Don't you see that what goes into the mouth can't defile a person, since it doesn't enter the heart but the stomach, and is sent into the latrine?

"But what comes out of the mouth proceeds from the heart, and this is what can defile a person.

"For from within comes evil thoughts, murder, sensuality, sexual immorality, adultery, coveting, theft, false witness, slander, deceit, envy, pride, foolishness, and wickedness.

"All these evil things come from within, and these are what defile a person. But to eat without performing the ritual hand-washing defiles no one." [61]

34

BROTHERLY ADVICE

THURSDAY, 15 SEPTEMBER AD 29, 10:00 AM

Once again John was here at the house where Jesus grew up in Nazareth. He had all of his first disciples with him: Peter, Andrew, Big James, John, Philip, and Nathanael.

The rest of the Twelve plus the female Four had gone ahead to Ephraim, along with Jesus' mother, Matthew's family, and Matthias. There they would rest at the home of Tad and his dad until next month's Festival of Booths in Jerusalem.

Jesus knocked on the front door, and his brother James — "James the Just" —opened the door. He said, "Well, if it isn't the Nazareth cat-burglar, who steals only food!"

Jesus grinned. "Hey, we paid well for the food we ate!"

James grinned back, saying, "Well, at least today you didn't sneak in by the back door! But tonight, your other brothers are coming over with their wives for a gourmet meal for all of us, courtesy of your oldest brother. And we'll have some more discussion about your career as a cat-burglar."

------•••●•••------

Gourmet it was, and John had eaten so much that he was stuffed. He said, "That was a great meal, James. Thank you!"

"Yes," James replied, "and now we can get down to what's been on our minds here in Nazareth. Jesus, you've been a stranger in Judea and Jerusalem for almost a year and a half now. We've thought that wasn't a really good idea for your new career as a prophet."

Youngest brother Jude said, "Yeah, we think that you should leave here, and go to Judea—at least for the Festival of Booths—so that your followers in Judea can see the works that you're doing. You could travel along with us and the family."

Brother Joseph said, "No one works in secret if he wants to be known openly."

Brother Simon said, "I agree. If you are doing all these astounding things, you should show yourself to the world."

Jesus said, "I appreciate your concern, but my time has not come yet. Your time is always here. The world can't hate you, but it hates me because I'm testifying that its works are evil.

"You guys go up to the festival. I'm not yet going to this festival, for my time has not yet fully come." [62]

* * *

John and Andrew were tucking themselves into their assigned beds, when Andrew said, "I don't think Jesus' brothers really believe in him, John."

John said, "I think they might just be on the fence, undecided yet. But at least they're not against him."

"You're right about that. They help him when they can, and they don't speak out against him."

"Yes, I'm glad about that. Goodnight, Andy."

"Goodnight, John."

35

SAMARITAN REJECTION

FRIDAY, 23 SEPTEMBER AD 29, 3:00 PM

John and Andrew were walking in the lead as they approached the Samaritan town of Ginae, but Big James was the first to see Nathanael and Philip coming towards them from town.

James said, "There they are! Now we'll find out what kind of lodging we'll have for tonight."

When the two lodging-scouts got close, Peter said, "What have you got for us, Nate?"

Nate said, "A whole lot of nothing, I'm afraid. When we asked about lodging, they asked us where we were headed. We said we were following Jesus, who has his face set toward Jerusalem."

Philip said, "The innkeeper said he knew of 'this man Jesus,' and he didn't want him in his town tearing down Samaria's high places of God. Then the merchants refused to sell us food or even a cup of their famous water."

Nate said, "We shook the dust off our feet against them."

James' face had been turning red and redder as they told their tale, and John was getting angry also.

James said to Jesus, "Lord, do you want us to call for fire to come down from heaven and burn them up?"

John said, "Yes, just like Elijah did!"

Jesus turned and faced the two brothers. He said, "You two really are Sons of Thunder, aren't you? Listen well: you do not know with what manner of spirit you are speaking. The Son of Man did not come to destroy people's lives, but to save them. Beware of anger, for with anger you give room for evil spirits to manipulate you."

There was silence for a moment. Then Peter said, "Well, what do we do now?"

Nate said, "There's another Samaritan town a few miles ahead: Bemesilis. We could get there by sunset."[63]

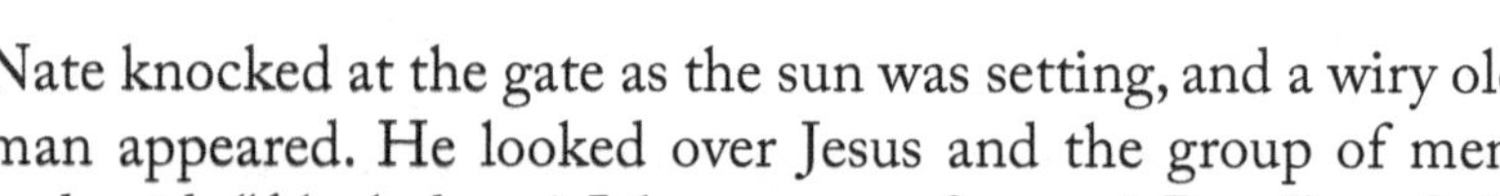

Nate knocked at the gate as the sun was setting, and a wiry old man appeared. He looked over Jesus and the group of men, and said, "Ah, lodgers! I have space for you! But I'm afraid you've missed dinner. I do have some bread left over and a few apricots and lots of well-water. Come on in!"

Jesus placed his hand on the doorpost and said, "Thank you, good sir. May God's peace be upon this house and all those who live here."

As the seven of them were settling in, John remembered a question he had meant to ask. He said, "Jesus, where are we going next? Jerusalem?"

Jesus said, "It is not quite time for that, John. For now, we'll be going beyond Jordan to bring the good news of the kingdom to the district of Perea. Then I'll be sending most of you to the Festival of Booths."

Peter said, "How will we keep in touch, Master?"

Jesus said, "You may pick up and leave messages at the home of Martha and Mary in Bethany. We will be in touch."

36

STUMBLING BLOCKS

Saturday, 1 October AD 29, 8:00 am

Jesus sat in the synagogue of Amathus in Perea with John standing behind him. In the assembly were two priests and several Pharisees from Jerusalem. John thought, "*Wow, those priests are not going to be happy with this scripture reading.*"

When it came time for the *haftarah*, Jesus stood up and John handed him the scroll of the prophet Malachi. Jesus unrolled the scroll and began to read:

> The lips of a priest should guard knowledge, and the people should seek learning from his mouth, for he is the messenger of the Lord of Heaven's Armies. But you priests have turned aside from the way! You have caused many to stumble by your teaching. The Lord of Heaven's Armies says to you, "You have fouled the covenant of priests, and so I will make you fouled and despised before the people, for you are not keeping my ways." [64]

Jesus gave the scroll back to John and sat down. All eyes in the assembly were on him, as he said, "Woe to you who cause

God's children to stumble, and give them temptations to do wrong! Temptations to sin are inevitable, but woe to him who does the tempting!

"Beside Jerusalem is the cursed valley of Gehenna, with its fire that cannot be quenched, and its maggots that never die. This represents the place where you will be cut off to reside forever, if you do not forsake your ways.

"So, if your hand causes you to sin, cut it off and throw it away! It is better for you to enter eternal life crippled than with both hands to go to Gehenna, where the fire cannot be quenched and the maggots never die.

"And if your foot causes you to sin, cut it off and throw it away! It is better for you to enter eternal life lame than with both feet to go to Gehenna, where the fire cannot be quenched and the maggots never die.

"And if your eye causes you to sin, tear it out and throw it away! It is better for you to enter eternal life with one eye than with two eyes to go to Gehenna, where the fire cannot be quenched and the maggots never die.

"Whoever has ears to hear, let him hear" [65]

When Jesus had finished these sayings, the synagogue service ended and he went outside, where a crowd was waiting for him. He healed many of them as they came forward with sickness and handicaps, and completely healed one man on the point of death who was carried to Jesus by his family.

The two priests walked out in a rage while the Pharisees indignantly watched Jesus healing on the Sabbath.

That night Jesus said, "Peter, tomorrow take James and Philip with you to Ephraim and join the Alpheus family. Andrew and Nathanael, go to Jerusalem to help Hezekiah build a booth for me. John, you will remain with me in Perea."

37

CHANGING BOOTH

SATURDAY, 15 OCTOBER AD 29, 5:00 AM

John awakened to Jesus' touch on his shoulder, and rolled over. Jesus said, "Eat some bread, my friend, it's going to be a long day: we're headed for the temple. Here's some dates and a piece of fruit for you."

John rubbed the sleep out of his eyes, and noted that it was still dark. They were in a small booth on a side street in the City of David, built by Hezekiah with some disciple help.

"Thanks, Teacher," said John. "I was talking with Hezzy last night, and he said people were looking for you on the second day of the festival, saying 'Where's Jesus?' Some were saying, 'He's a good man,' and others said, 'No, he's leading the people astray.' But they're all just muttering, because they don't want the Pharisees to hear them talking about you."

Jesus said, "Don't worry about them; they'll have plenty to say about me after today. Put on your cape with the hood and bring your pack along; we're going to Solomon's Colonnade."

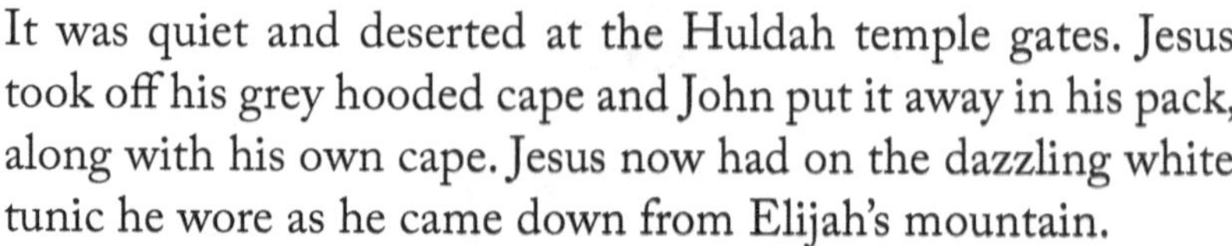

It was quiet and deserted at the Huldah temple gates. Jesus took off his grey hooded cape and John put it away in his pack, along with his own cape. Jesus now had on the dazzling white tunic he wore as he came down from Elijah's mountain.

When he and John reached Solomon's Colonnade, the rest of the Twelve plus a dozen other disciples were already there, waiting in the faint light of the new dawn.

Jesus immediately began teaching about the kingdom of God. Within a few minutes, he had attracted a dozen passersby, and before long two Pharisees came over to find out what was going on.

The first one said, "Isn't this the man who was healing on the Sabbath two weeks ago in Amathus? He should be ashamed."

The second one said, "How is it that this man knows the sacred scriptures, when he has never studied in a school?"

Jesus answered them, "This teaching is not mine, but comes from the one who sent me. If anyone wants to do God's will, he will know whether the teaching is from God or whether I'm speaking on my own authority. The one who seeks the glory of him who sent him is true, and there is no falsehood in him.

"Hasn't Moses given you the Law? Yet none of you keeps the law. Why do you seek to kill me?"

A voice from the gathering crowd said, "You have a demon! Who is seeking to kill you?"

Jesus said, "I did one work in Amathus, and you all marvel at it. Moses gave you circumcision, and you circumcise a man on the Sabbath. If on the Sabbath a man is circumcised so that the law may not be broken, why are you angry with me because I made a man's whole body well on the Sabbath? Do not judge by appearances, but judge correctly."

The two Pharisees left, and went into the temple for the morning rituals. The crowd around Jesus had grown larger, and some were murmuring. John heard one man say, "Isn't this the man that the chief priests want to kill? But here he is, speaking openly, and they say nothing to him! Could it be that they know this is really the Messiah?"

Another man replied, "No, but we know where this man comes from—a little village in Galilee. When the Messiah appears, no one will know where he comes from."

Jesus said, "You do know me, and where I come from. But I have not come on my own accord. The one who sent me is true, and him you do not know. I know him, for I came from him, and he sent me."

The second man said, "I've had enough. I'm going to get the temple police to put a stop to this." The man went into the temple, but no police came out. Instead, four more Pharisees came from the temple to listen.

Yet as Jesus continued teaching, many began to believe in him. Some said, "When the Messiah appears, will he do more signs and wonders than this man has done?"

An hour passed, and the Pharisees returned to the temple, vowing that Jesus would be arrested. After a few minutes, the captain of the guard came out with two temple police to investigate, followed by the Pharisees.

By this time there were some two hundred people surrounding Jesus as he taught. The officers were unable to get past the throng standing around Jesus, and were reluctant to draw their swords.

On seeing the officers, Jesus said to the crowd, "I will be with you a little longer, and then I'm going to the one who sent me. You'll look for me, but you won't find me. Where I'm going you cannot come."

One of the Pharisees said, "Where will this man go that we won't find him? To the Jews in other countries? To the Greeks? And what does he mean, 'You'll look for me but not find me,' and 'Where I am you can't come'?" [66]

Hours passed, and evening dimmed the sky. There was still a crowd around Jesus, but he began working his way through them and over to the latrine just outside the sheep gate—along with the entire Twelve. John and Jesus donned their hooded cloaks, and exited by another gate. In the confusion, they were easily able to arrive at the Huldah gates with no one noticing them.

John said, "We got out of there! And you didn't get arrested!"

Jesus said, "Yes, my Father knows what he's doing. But as you know, the temple police have orders not to risk starting a riot. They'll have to find some other way to arrest me. Some day they will, but this is not that day."

38

PROPHET FROM GALILEE

It was the last day of the festival, the great day. John took Jesus' cloak from him, and it appeared as if Jesus had just stepped out of nowhere, into the middle of the temple itself.

Jesus stood up and cried out, "If anyone thirsts, let him come to me and drink! Whoever believes in me, let him come to me, and let him who believes in me drink! As the scripture has said, 'Out of his heart will flow rivers of living water.' I will pour out water on the thirsty, and I will pour out my spirit on your offspring." [67]

When the people heard these words, some of them said, "This has to be the promised Prophet." But others said, "No, no! This is the Messiah."

But a teacher of the Law said, "Does the Messiah really come from Galilee? Doesn't scripture say the Messiah comes from David's offspring, and will be born in Bethlehem, David's village?"

That started an argument amid the temple. Some men yelled, "Prophet!" and others shouted "Messiah!" And the loudest ones howled, "Arrest him!" But Jesus was not to be found. He had stepped behind a wall of disciples, and with John's help, disappeared.

***

"John?"

"*Who's using my name out loud?*" John looked out of the booth to find out.

"John! It was tough to find you!"

John stepped out of the booth and said quietly, "Elnathan! Yes, I'm here, but don't use my name out loud here. The neighbors are already wondering who we are."

More quietly, Elnathan said, "Is Jesus here?"

"Yes, but he's asleep. How did you find us?"

"I went to Hezekiah. He made me swear an oath of secrecy before he would tell me."

"It's good to see you, but what brings you here today?"

"I'm bringing you an update. The chief priests and the Supreme Council have been really agitated the last few days."

"Oh, I'd love to hear. I'm sure we've been poking a stick in their ribs."

"That's a good way to put it. When the officers they sent out to arrest Jesus came back without him, the high priest said, 'Why didn't you bring him here?' and the captain said, "No one ever spoke like this man!"

"Oh, wow."

"Yes, the high priest turned as red as a beet, saying things like 'Are you also deceived?' and 'Have any of us ever believed him?' and 'You've let this accursed crowd sway you.' I was standing right there when he said these things."

"Hah! That must have been really entertaining."

"Yes, but here's the best part: when the chief priests met with the Pharisees, Nicodemus defended Jesus to their face."

"Oh! What did he say?"

"He said, "Does our law judge a man without giving him a hearing and learning what he does?"

John said, "So, what did the chief priests say?"

"They said, 'Are you from Galilee too?' and 'No prophet rises out of Galilee!' But I think they slipped up there." [68]

"You're right. The prophet Jonah was born west of the sea of Kinnereth, which we now call Galilee. It's disgraceful that a high priest should make such a mistake."

Elnathan said, "Yes, his disciples know Jesus was born in Bethlehem, not far from here. And some of the crowds are starting to learn this also."

"I'm glad you came by, Elnathan. Are you still gonna stick with Nicodemus?"

"I really wanna get away and hang with Jesus and you guys. But for the next few months it's gonna be really important for you to know what the Supreme Council is up to. Nicodemus really wants to help Jesus."

"This is great stuff you're doing, guy. But watch your back. I'm pretty sure your life would be in danger if they found out you were spying for Jesus."

"You're probably right. But John?"

"Yes?"

"You guys really have the full attention of Caiaphas the high priest right now."

"I'll bet we do. Take care, Elnathan. Hezekiah and I will be tearing this booth down today, and I'll be over at his house for a couple days."

"Okay. You take care also, John."

39

THOMAS WORRIES

FRIDAY, 21 OCTOBER AD 29, 9:00 AM

The Festival of Booths was over, and the crowds were thinning out. Jesus was visiting his friends in Bethany, and John was napping in the room above Hezekiah's mud hut. He woke to voices in the alley below.

"John! Are you in there?"

John rolled off his sleeping mat and looked out the window to see Philip and Thomas below. "Hi, guys, come on up!"

As they came in the door, John said, "What brings you men over here today?"

Philip said, "We didn't have any assignments to do this day, so we thought we'd look around. Thomas hadn't seen Hezekiah's place."

Thomas said, "Yeah. It's humble, but it looks structurally sound. It's not going to fall in on us."

John said, "Are you an expert in such things? "

"Yeah, sorta. I was in training to be an architect,[69] but my instructor died when I still had a year to go in my schooling."

"Oh, that's interesting. How did you get started in that?

"It's a long, sad story, I'm afraid."

"Tell me more; we've got all day."

Thomas said, "My twin brother died when a wall fell on him during an earthquake. We were 10 years old, and the wall had not been built properly. My Dad vowed to become an architect and design walls that wouldn't fall.

John said, "Oh, I'm sorry. Did your dad go to a school?"

"Yes, he went to Athens in Greece where the top experts could be found. When he came back, he trained me how to speak Greek correctly."

Philip said, "Thomas and I have been going around to the Greek-speaking synagogues to spread the good news."

Thomas said, "Yes, that's one of the legacies my father left to me. He was training me to be an architect, but he died when we were barely getting started."

John said, "Wow. What did you do then?"

"My family was poor, so they looked for a way to enroll me as an understudy to an architect here. They finally found one in Sepphoris that would accept me, an older man that was getting ready to retire. But he was not a Jew."

"Was that a problem?"

"Not at first, but when he died it was a problem. The Jewish architects wouldn't take me because I had been studying with a pagan, and the pagan architects wouldn't take me because I was a Jew. Nobody wanted me."

Philip said, "But Jesus wanted you."

"Yes, and I'll always be grateful for that. But he's getting ready to die too, and I'll be alone again. My twin brother died, my father died, my teacher died, and now Jesus is going to die. It feels like I'm under a curse. It might be better for me if I died with him."

"Oh! Don't say that!" said John. "Jesus says that he's bringing us everlasting life!"

"Yes, I really want to believe that," said Thomas. "But I'm struggling. It feels like death is stalking me."

John said, "I say it's more like a demon that wants to take you out. But you're under the protection of Jesus, our great savior, dead or alive. That demon doesn't have a chance."

40

BORN BLIND

John arrived at the inn in the Upper City where he and Andrew and Nathanael had first stayed with Tad and his father Little James, the Levite. He stepped up to the door as James himself was walking out.

John said, "James! There you are!"

James said, "Hi, John. Good to see you! Come on up to the room where we're staying."

John followed James to a room where some 20 disciples were talking and eating. They shouted out, "HI, JOHN!"

John said, "Hi, guys! Hey, tomorrow Jesus is going to the Synagogue of Hillel, right near here. A lot of the Pharisees hang out there. He wants some of you to come along for the morning Sabbath service."

Andrew said, "Oh, wow. Hillel, the greatest rabbi, the one who used to argue with rabbi Shammai."

Thaddeus said, "I heard there's a big chair there they won't let anyone use, because Hillel used to sit in it and teach."

Nathanael said, "I doubt that. Rabbi Hillel died twenty years ago, and this synagogue was built in his honor ten years after that.[70] But I do think Nicodemus attends there."

Little James said, "That's true, Nate, but he's only there once in a while."

Philip said, "Was Jesus invited to speak?"

John said, "I don't think so. That would be quite an event."

Big James said, "We might be thrown out as soon as they see us."

Thomas said, "Oh, that would be interesting. I'm sure Jesus would have some choice words for them then."

Nathanael chuckled. "We can tell them, 'Well, we'll just go over to the Synagogue of Shammai instead.'"

Everybody laughed.

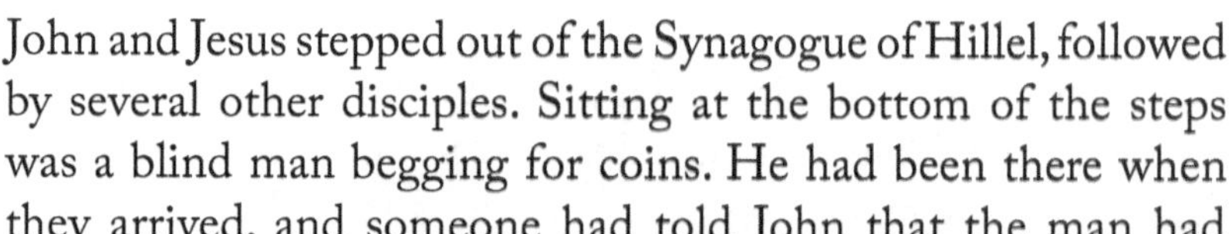

John and Jesus stepped out of the Synagogue of Hillel, followed by several other disciples. Sitting at the bottom of the steps was a blind man begging for coins. He had been there when they arrived, and someone had told John that the man had been blind from birth.

John asked Jesus, "Teacher, why was this man born blind? Did he sin? Or did his parents sin?"

Jesus said, "He was not born blind because of his sin, nor because of his parents' sin. No, this took place so that the mighty works of God might be displayed in him. We must do the work of the one who sent me while it is still day. Night is coming, when no one can work. But as long as I am in the world, I am the light of day for the world."

Jesus said to the man, "Tell me your name."

He said, "They call me Nicanor."

Jesus then bent down and spit on the ground. He made some mud with the saliva and anointed the man's eyes with the mud.

He said to the blind man, "Nicanor, go, I am sending you. Wash in the pool of Siloam."[71]

41

I Am

Sunday, 23 October AD 29, 6:00 AM

John woke in the room above Hezekiah's house and looked out the window. The neighborhood was quiet and there was no traffic in the street.

Hezekiah's mom Abigail would soon send up one of the boys with food for John and Jesus to eat, and then John would follow Jesus to Solomon's Colonnade.

They were no longer hiding themselves when they travelled the streets of Jerusalem. It seemed like the temple police had excused themselves from trying to arrest Jesus. Jesus said it was just not his time yet.

But they were still careful when leaving or returning to Hezekiah's house. If their presence became known, there would be a crowd at the stairs every day, filling the street.

The families of the disciples who came for the festival had left for home days ago. But several of the disciples had been sent out on a mission. Using Joseph *bar* Sabba's list, they were fanning out into Judea and Galilee to summon the roll call of Jesus' traveling disciples. Jesus said the harvest was ready, and workers were needed.

Jesus came to the window behind John. He said, "It's peaceful out there, John."

John said, "Yes, teacher. But soon the younger children will be playing outside, and the older ones with Hezekiah will go out on their scavenging run. They have been doing well."

Jesus said, "Yes, my Father has been blessing them. Remember I said that whoever gives you even a cup of cold water will not lose his reward."

———•••●•••———

John stood beside Jesus at Solomon's Colonnade. Some Pharisees opposed to Jesus had gathered and Jesus was revisiting some of the teachings he had given yesterday. Ten of Jesus' disciples stood nearby in case there was danger to Jesus.

The crowd moved in closer. Jesus said, "If you abide in my word, you are truly my disciples, and you will know the truth, and the truth will set you free." Some nodded in agreement.

But a tall man said, "We've never been slaves!"

Jesus said, "Truly I tell you, everyone who practices sin is a slave to sin. A slave does not remain forever, but the son does remain forever. So if the Son sets you free, you will be free indeed. I speak of my Father, but you follow your father."

The tall man said, "Abraham is my father!"

Jesus said, "If so, you would be doing what Abraham did. But you seek to kill me because I told you the truth."

Several of them said, "We have one Father—even God!"

Jesus said, "If that were true, you would love me, for I came from God. I didn't come on my own, but God sent me to you. But you are of your father the devil, and your will is to do your father's desires.

"There is no truth in the devil. He is a liar and the father of lies. But because I tell the truth, you don't believe me. Truly,

truly I say to you, if any of you keep my word, he will never see death."

The tall man said, "Now we know you have a demon! Abraham died, and all the prophets, but you say we won't die if we keep your word? Who do you think you are?

Jesus said, "Abraham rejoiced that he would see my day. He saw it and was glad."

The man said, "You're not even fifty years old, and you say Abraham has seen you? How can that be?"

Jesus raised his voice and said, "*Truly I tell you, before Abraham was, I am.*"

Several men began picking up stones to throw at Jesus, but his disciples gathered around him, and he slipped away.[72]

42

THE BLIND SEE

WEDNESDAY, 26 OCTOBER AD 29, 8:00 AM

There was a knock on the upper room door, and John opened it. He said, "Nate! What brings you? Come in."

Nathanael stepped in, and Jesus said, "Welcome! What news have you brought me?"

Nate said, "Teacher, I just came from Nicanor, the blind man that you healed on the Sabbath. He's been cast out of the synagogue."

"Ah," said Jesus, "Tell us the story."

"Nicanor found someone to lead him by the hand, and went as you instructed to the Pool of Siloam. He washed and became able to see. When he went home, his neighbors hardly knew it was him, but he kept saying, 'I am Nicanor, and I can see now!' He told them that a man called Jesus healed him, but he didn't know where the man went after that.

"So they took him to the Pharisees of his own synagogue, because he had been healed on the Sabbath. He told them how this Jesus healed him, and they replied that this man was not of God, for he fails to keep the Sabbath. But others said, 'How can a sinner do such signs?'

"Then the Pharisees called his parents, because the Pharisees didn't believe he was blind and now could see. They asked them how the man gained his sight, but his parents were afraid that if they told, they would be put out of the synagogue.

"So they called for Nicanor again, to try to shake his story. By this time Nicanor had enough of their foolishness, and he told them that Jesus is a prophet from God. He said, 'If this man were not from God, he could do nothing.'

"The Pharisees were offended that Nicanor was trying to teach them something, so they banned him from the synagogue."

Jesus said, "Take me to Nicanor."

Nathanael led Jesus and John through Jerusalem to Nicanor's house. Two Pharisees spotted Jesus on the streets of the Upper City, and followed. When Jesus found Nicanor, he said, "Do you believe in the Son of Man?"

Nicanor answered, "And who is he, sir, that I may believe in him?"

Jesus said, "You have seen him, and it is he who is speaking to you."

Nicanor said, "My Lord, I believe."

Jesus said, "For judgment such as this I came into this world, so that those who do not see may see, and those who see may become blind."

One of the Pharisees standing there said to Jesus, "Does this mean that we also are blind?"

Jesus said, "If you were blind, you would not have sin. But since you say, 'We see,' your guilt remains." [73]

43

· ·

GOOD SHEPHERD

Nathanael said, "We're gonna need more housing."

John replied, "Yeah, last time we were in Gibeah there were something like forty of us in this room, and it was packed."

Simon the Zealot said, "We're gonna have more than double that number by this time next week. I'm getting good reports back from the crew that went out to bring in the disciples."

Judas of Kerioth said, "This is gonna cost an arm and a leg. I've got money in the moneybag but I don't know how long it'll hold out."

John said, "I'm guessing that right after next Sabbath we'll start clearing out of here."

Peter said, "Nate, why don't you and Simon start checking with the neighbors? Everyone should be gone from the festival by now, so there's bound to be room somewhere."

Simon said, "Will do, boss. I can start by checking with the folks that come to synagogue this morning."

Nate said, "It's gonna be crowded there today. The Pharisees got wind of our move to Gibeah, and there's gonna be some of them here to contradict whatever Jesus says."

"Jesus can handle it," said Thomas.

Jesus stood up, and John handed the scroll of Ezekiel to him. He unrolled it, and began to read:

> The word of the Lord came to me: "Son of man, prophesy against the shepherds of Israel; say to the shepherds, 'Thus says the Lord God: "Ah, shepherds of Israel who have been feeding yourselves! Should not shepherds feed the sheep? You eat the fat, you clothe yourselves with the wool, you slaughter the fat ones, but you do not feed the sheep.
>
> The weak you have not strengthened, the sick you have not healed, the injured you have not bound up, the strayed you have not brought back, the lost you have not sought, and with force and harshness you have ruled them. So they were scattered, because there was no shepherd, and they became food for all the wild beasts.'"
>
> For thus says the Lord God: "Behold, I myself will search for my sheep and will seek them out. As a shepherd seeks out his flock when he is among his sheep that have been scattered, so will I seek out my sheep, and I will rescue them from all places where they have been scattered in clouds and thick darkness." [74]

Jesus gave the scroll back to John, and sat down. He said, "Truly I say to you, the one who does not enter the sheepfold by the door but climbs in another way is a thief. But he who enters by the door is the shepherd of the sheep. To him the gatekeeper opens.

"The sheep hear his voice, and he calls them by name and leads them out. He goes before them, and the sheep follow him because they know his voice. They won't follow a stranger, but run from him for they do not know the stranger's voice. Do you understand this?"

Someone called out, "Who's the shepherd?"

Jesus said, "Truly I say to you, I am the door of the sheep. All who came before me are thieves, but the sheep didn't listen to them. I am the door. If anyone enters by me, he will be saved and will find pasture.

"I am the good shepherd. I know my own and my own know me, just as the Father knows me and I know the Father. I lay down my life for the sheep.

"I have other sheep that are not of this fold. I must bring them also, and they will listen to my voice. So there will be one flock and one shepherd.

"For this reason the Father loves me, because I lay down my life that I may take it up again. No one takes it from me; I lay it down of my own accord. I have authority to lay it down and take it up again. This charge I received from my Father."

The leader of the synagogue called for a psalm to be sung, and closed the meeting in prayer, as a murmur of conversation spread across the assembly.

John saw that some of the usual Pharisees were there. One of them said, "He's insane, why listen to him?"

Another agreed, "He has a demon, that's for sure."

But a third one said, "These aren't the words of someone who has a demon. Can a demon open the eyes of the blind?"[75]

44

SEVENTY SENT

TUESDAY, 7 NOVEMBER AD 29, 7:00 AM

John came down the steps from the upper room and found Simon the Zealot and Joseph *bar* Sabbas huddled over several pieces of parchment with notes on them.

John said, "Hi, guys. Are those the roll-call notes?"

Simon said, "Yeah. We had a good turnout. There's one more, Seth *ben* Salmon. He said he was coming, but he hasn't shown up yet."

John said, "How many have checked in?"

Joseph said, "Well, besides the Twelve, and the fifteen that walked with Jesus when the Twelve were sent out, I'm counting seventy-two that have checked in here, for a total of ninety-nine."

"I thought there were a lot more disciples than that," said John.

Joseph said, "There are, but these are the ones who have actually walked with Jesus when he was travelling and teaching. There are lots more that have pledged their belief in Jesus, more than I can count. We only have the names of a couple hundred of them."

Simon said, "This guy Seth has missed all the training sessions that Jesus has been giving in the plaza."

John said, "Well, Jesus is giving the final training session at noon today. He's going to send them out into the harvest, like he did with the Twelve."

It was time for the big meeting, and Gibeah's central plaza was filled with Jesus' disciples. Many of the townspeople and other onlookers stood around the edge.

Jesus climbed a large rock at the center of the plaza, while John and Peter stood on the ground beside it. Just as Jesus was about to speak, a man came jostling through the crowd saying, "Wait, wait!"

When the man reached Jesus he said, "Master, I am Seth *ben* Salmon, and I have come, for you have called. I will follow you, Lord, but please allow me to first say goodbye to my family at home."

Jesus said, "Seth, I know you, but no one who puts his hand to the plow and then looks back is ready to serve the kingdom of God. You are excused; go back to your family." [76]

The man's face was crestfallen as he made his way out of the plaza.

Jesus stood up to speak to his disciples. He said, "The harvest is plentiful, but the workers are few. So pray intensely to the Lord of the harvest to send out workers into his fields.

"You are the Seventy-Two; I am sending you out ahead of me, two by two, to prepare the way for the Son of Man. Listen! I am sending you as lambs into the midst of wolves. But carry no moneybag, no pack, no extra sandals, and greet no one on the road.

"When you enter a house, say 'Peace be upon this house!' If a son of peace lives there, your peace will rest on him. But if not, it will return to you. Stay in the same house, and eat and drink whatever they provide, for the worker deserves his wages. Do not go from house to house.

"When you enter a town and they receive you, heal the sick and tell them, 'The kingdom of God has come near to you. But if you enter a town and they do not receive you, go in the street and say, 'Even the dust of your town on our feet we wipe off against you.' I tell you, on that great day it will be more bearable for Sodom than for that town.

"Anyone who hears you hears me, and anyone who rejects you rejects me. And whoever rejects me rejects the one who sent me." [77]

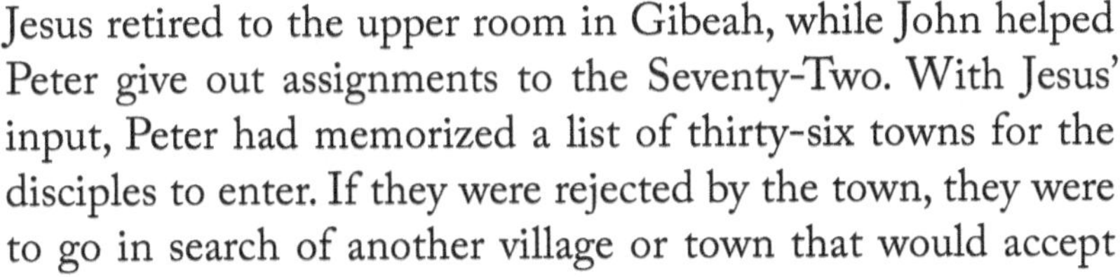

Jesus retired to the upper room in Gibeah, while John helped Peter give out assignments to the Seventy-Two. With Jesus' input, Peter had memorized a list of thirty-six towns for the disciples to enter. If they were rejected by the town, they were to go in search of another village or town that would accept them.

When the last assignment had been given, John said, "Simon, almost all those towns are in Judea."

Peter said, "I know. Jesus wants to visit every one of the towns and villages in Judea, but he said there is no time left to finish the job. Then he said something strange."

John said, "Oh, what?"

"He said that his disciples will have to finish the job after the Son of Man is raised up."

"I wonder what that means."

45

SAMARITAN NEIGHBOR

SATURDAY, 12 NOVEMBER AD 29, 8:00 AM

The leader of the synagogue in Gibeah had invited Jesus to speak again because, as he told John, "I like having the synagogue full to the walls."

So here John was again, receiving the scroll from Jesus, who sat down and said, "O Judah! O Israel! That you would only repent and turn back to God! Then you would receive the eternal joy promised through the word of Isaiah!"[78]

There was silence in the room.

Then a teacher of the Law stood up, and—surprise—it was a Pharisee, the one who had defended Jesus against the charge of having a demon. He said, "Teacher, what must I do to receive eternal life?"

Jesus said, "Tell me, what is written in the Law? How do you read it?"

He said, "You shall love the Lord your God with all your heart and with all your soul and with all your mind, and your neighbor as yourself."

Jesus said, "You have answered correctly. Do this, and you will live."[79]

And then he asked, "But who is my neighbor?"

"Listen well: A man was going down from Jerusalem to Jericho, and robbers fell upon him, stripping him and beating him. The robbers left him there half dead.

"Now by chance a priest was going down that road, and when he saw him he passed by on the other side of the road. Likewise a Levite, who came to that place and saw him, passed by on the other side. But a traveling Samaritan came by and saw him. and had compassion for him.

"He went to him and bound up his wounds, pouring on oil and wine. Then he set him on his own donkey and brought him to an inn and took care of him that night.

"The next day he took out two denarii and gave them to the innkeeper. He told him, 'Take care of this man, and whatever more you spend, I will repay you when I come back.'

"Now which of these three, do you think, proved to be a neighbor to the man who was fallen upon by robbers?"

The Pharisee said, "I suppose it was the one who showed him mercy."

And Jesus said, "You go, and do likewise." [80]

46

. . . .

MARTHA AND MARY

MONDAY, 20 NOVEMBER AD 29, 4:00 PM

John shouldered his pack. He said, "Come on, Andrew, you're behind. We're going to Martha and Mary's."

Andrew found his cloak, and stuffed it into his pack. They were the last ones to leave; all the rest were on their way out of Gibeah. "Okay, I think I have everything," he said. "How did we get invited?"

John said, "Simon the Leper, the disciple that Jesus healed two years ago, came over with the invitation from Martha. She's gonna feed all of us. Well, not all, mostly those of the Twelve that are still here, plus Concordia and the Magdalene."

Andrew said, "Who left?"

"Well as you know, Matthew and Matt went home to see their family. Tad and his dad are here, and probably his dad's brother Joses, but I think the Zealot and the Keriothite have gone down to Hebron. Oh, and Matthias is with us."

"What about the rest? I know that Perez is here."

"Yeah, he found a place to stay in the lower city near the Essene gate with *bar* Sabbas and Gemariah and Tobias. The others have gone to Galilee."

John and Andrew were the last to arrive in Bethany, as the streets began to darken. John knocked at the door, and Lazarus answered it. "John! Andrew! There you are! Martha was worrying about you. Welcome!"

Martha was bustling around preparing food, and Lazarus was carrying things back and forth to set the table. Some of Martha and Mary's friends were there, and Jesus was repeating the parable of the Samaritan Neighbor for them, while Mary sat at Jesus' feet listening.

John was hungry, and kept looking at the kitchen door expecting food to come out.

Jesus had almost finished his tale of the Samaritan, when Martha came into the room and approached Jesus. Jesus looked up at Martha.

Martha said, "Lord, don't you care that my sister has left me to serve alone? Tell her to help me."

Jesus smiled. He said, "Martha, Martha. You are anxious and troubled about many things, but just one thing is needed. Mary has chosen the good portion, and it will not be taken away from her."[81]

Martha thought about that, then turned to go back to the kitchen. Concordia and Mary Magdalene got up to follow her, and the Magdalene said, "Is there anything we can do to help?"

Martha said, "Oh, no, you are guests tonight. Go sit down and relax."

Concordia said, "Oh, no, we're not going to have any of that tonight. You're getting helpers whether you want them or not."

Martha teared up, and hugged Concordia. She said, "Thanks, girlfriend. I needed that."

47

HOW TO PRAY

WEDNESDAY, 23 NOVEMBER AD 29, 6:00 AM

John, Andrew, Peter, and James were together with Jesus on a hilltop, for Jesus had roused them this morning before dawn and led them up to the Mount of Olives to pray. John was done praying, so he was watching the dawn sweep the night away.

Jesus was a stone's throw away. He finished praying and came over to the disciples.

John said, "Master, would you teach us to pray, like John the Baptist taught his disciples?"

Jesus sat down and said, "When you come before the Father, pray like this:

> Our Father in heaven
> Let your name be holy.
> Let your kingdom come.
> Let your will be done,
>   on earth as it is in heaven.
> Give us each day our daily bread,

And forgive us our trespasses,
    as we forgive those who have
    trespassed against us.
And do not put us to the test,
    but deliver us from the evil one.

Jesus continued, saying, "For if you forgive others their trespasses, your Father in heaven will also forgive you. But if you do not forgive others, then neither will you be forgiven.

"But don't be like the hypocrites. They love to stand and pray in the synagogue or on street corners, so they can be seen by others. Truly I tell you, they already have their reward.

"However, when you pray, go into your room and shut the door, praying to your Father in secret. Your Father who sees you in secret will reward you.

"And when you pray, don't repeat empty phrases as the idol-worshippers do, for they think they will be heard by heaping up many words. Don't be like them, for your Father knows what you need before you ask him.

"So, which of you who has a friend will go to him at midnight and knock at his door saying, 'Friend, loan me three loaves of bread, for I have a guest who just arrived on a journey, and I have nothing to give him.' What will he do?"

James said, "He'd tell me to just go away."

Jesus answered, "Yes, he will call back to you, 'Don't bother me! My door is shut and my children are with me in bed. I can't get up and give you anything!'"

James said, "Yup, that would be the friend I'm thinking of."

Jesus said, "Ah, but I tell you that even though he won't get up just because you're his friend, yet if you are persistent he will arise and give you whatever you need."

"Ask, and it will be given to you; seek, and you will find; knock, and it will be opened to you. For the one who asks receives, and the one who seeks finds, and to the one who knocks it will be opened.

"If a son asks for bread, what father will give him a stone? Or if he asks for a fish, give him a serpent; or for an egg, give him a scorpion? If you who are evil know how to give good gifts to your children, how much more will the heavenly Father give to those who ask of him!" [82]

48

WOE!

Sunday, 27 November AD 29, 4:00 PM

John looked at the sumptuous meal that was laid out before him, and salivated as Jesus said the blessing:

Blessed are you, Father, King of the Universe, who brings forth bread from the earth!

John was seated at a side table by the wall, and was right behind Jesus who was reclining at the main table in the center of the room, having been invited by the Pharisee who had defended Jesus.

Next to Jesus sat the Pharisee at the head of the table, with his friends reclining beside him. Nathanael and Matthias were there also, at the same table as John.

Jesus and the disciples began eating, for set before them was savory roast pheasant. Their Pharisee-friend looked surprised. He said to Jesus, "Teacher, I am astonished that you and your disciples did not ritually wash your hands before eating! Why is that?"

Jesus said, "There is no defilement that comes upon a man because he does not ritually wash. You Pharisees have many practices like this. You clean the outside of the cup and the dish, while inside you are full of greed and wickedness.

"You fools! Didn't he who made the outside make the inside also? Woe to you Pharisees! For you give as an offering a tenth of the mint you grow in your window-gardens, and a tenth of the herbs, while you neglect justice and the love of God. This you should do, without neglecting the others.

"Woe to you Pharisees! For you cherish the best seats in the synagogues and honorable greetings in the marketplaces. "Woe to you! For you are like unmarked graves, that defile those that walk over them without knowing it."

One of the Pharisees said, "Teacher, in saying these things you also insult the teachers of the Law."

Jesus said, "Woe also to you teachers of the Law! For you load people down with unbearable burdens, and you yourselves do not lift a finger to lighten their loads.

"Woe to you! For you build the tombs of the prophets that were killed by your fathers. In this way you are witnesses who consent to the deeds of your fathers, for they killed them, and you build their tombs.

"Therefore God in his wisdom said, 'I will send them prophets and apostles, some of whom they will kill and persecute.' Therefore, this generation will be held responsible for the blood of all the prophets shed from the beginning of the world, even from the blood of Abel to the blood of Zechariah, who you killed between the sanctuary and the altar. Truly I tell you, this generation will be held responsible for it all"

"Woe to you experts in the Law! You have taken away the keys of knowledge. You did not enter yourselves, and you held back those who were entering. Woe to you!"

•◦●◦◦•

As the disciples departed after the meal, Nathanael said to John, "I heard some murmuring in there: some of the Pharisees and teachers of the Law are going to look for a way to trip Jesus up, to get their revenge on him." [83]

49

. . . .

FIVE SPARROWS

WEDNESDAY, 30 NOVEMBER AD 29, 8:00 AM

John and the disciples were walking with Jesus from Bethany to the temple, about two miles distant. Jesus had been teaching at the colonnade for two days now, and the crowds were starting to become massive. Many believed in him, and drew in close to hear.

John was walking beside Nathanael. He said, "Nate, you were right about the Pharisees and Teachers of the Law. They've been making catcalls and interruptions, but Jesus has started to ignore them."

"You're right, John. He's been directing his teaching to the ones that believe in him. More of the Pharisees are starting to draw away from him, but they haven't been able to discredit him with the people."

John said, "I don't think they will, either. But they're sure annoying."

———— •••●••• ————

John kept his station beside Jesus, in case Jesus wanted or needed anything, or a message sent. Jesus began speaking, and the noise of the crowd settled down. He called out loudly, "For you who believe, beware of the leaven of the Pharisees, the leaven of hypocrisy. Nothing is covered up that will not be exposed, or concealed that will not be known.

"Therefore, whatever you have said in the dark shall be heard in the light, and what you have whispered in private rooms shall be shouted from the rooftops.

"I tell you, my friends, do not fear those who can kill the body, and that is all they can do. I'll tell you who to fear: Fear the one who, after he has killed, has the authority to throw your soul into Gehenna, where the fire does not go out and the maggots never die. Yes, I say, fear him!

"Aren't five sparrows sold for two lepta? [84] And not even one sparrow is forgotten before God. For you, my friends, even the hairs of your head have been numbered. Fear not; you are more valuable than many sparrows.

"I tell you the truth, everyone who acknowledges me before men, the Son of Man will also acknowledge before the angels of God. But the one who denies me before men will be denied before the angels of God.

"So when they bring you before the synagogues to be cast out, or the temple rulers to be ostracized, or the Roman authorities to be punished, do not be anxious about how you should defend yourself or what you should say. In that very hour the Holy Spirit will teach you what you ought to say." [85]

———•••●•••———

"By my guess, more than a thousand people came today to hear Jesus," said Joseph *bar* Sabbas."

"Yeah, I'm glad you're here to watch the crowd," said John. "I wish the Zealot was back. He's good at finding out what's going on in these crowds."

50

FEAR NOT, LITTLE FLOCK

"The crowd is even bigger today," said Andrew.

Nathanael said, "I'd say there's more than two thousand. And the way the crowd builds, there'll be three thousand by noon. I hope we don't see anyone trampled."

John said, "Are most of them believers?"

Philip said, "I think so. The ones against Jesus hang around the edge of the crowd mostly."

James said, "I'm sticking close to Jesus for his safety. I wish the Zealot was here."

Peter said, "He'll be here by the Sabbath. And Jesus won't be teaching on the colonnade tomorrow."

John said, "Then we'll get some rest."

———— ·•●●•· ————

Jesus stepped in front of the column where he had been teaching, and the crowd started to settle down. Then someone in the crowd yelled, "Teacher, tell my brother to divide the inheritance with me!"

Jesus said, "Man, who set me up as a judge or an arbitrator between you?"

Then he said to the crowd, "Take care, and be on guard against all greediness, for a person's life does not consist in the abundance of his possessions.

"Listen! There was a rich man whose land produced abundantly. He thought to himself, 'What shall I do, for I don't have enough room to store all my crops?'

"And he said, 'I know! I will tear down my barns and build larger ones, and there I can store all my grain and goods. And I will say to my soul, "Soul, you have plenty of goods laid up for many years. Relax, eat, drink, and be merry"'

"But God said to him, 'Fool! This very night your soul is required of you, and as for these goods, whose will they be?'

"So it will be with the one who lays up treasure for himself and is not rich toward God. And you, my disciples, listen well.

"Don't be anxious about what you will eat or what you will wear. Life is more than food, and the body more than clothing.

"Consider the ravens: they don't sow seeds, they don't harvest crops, they have no storehouses or barns, and yet God feeds them. How much more valuable are you than the birds!

"And which one of you, by being anxious, can add a single hour to his lifespan? If you're unable to do as small a thing as that, why are you anxious about the rest?

"Consider the lilies, how they grow: They don't spin or weave, yet I tell you even Solomon in his glory wasn't dressed like one of these. But if God so clothes the grass, which is alive today in the field, and is thrown tomorrow into the oven, how much more will he clothe you, O you of little faith!

"Don't run after food and drink, for all the nations run after them, but your Father knows you need them. Instead, seek your Father's kingdom, and these things will be added to you.

"Fear not, little flock, for it is your Father's good pleasure to give you the kingdom. Sell your possessions, and give to the needy. Provide yourselves lasting treasure in heaven, where no thief comes near and no moth destroys. For where your treasure is, there your heart will be also." [86]

51

STAY READY

MONDAY, 5 DECEMBER AD 29, 8:00 AM

"Hi, Matt, glad you're back! You guys staying at the leper's house?"

"Yeah, me and Matthias and the Bashan brothers. Amram wanted to come too, but mom said he had to wait till he was thirteen to go 'gallivanting around' as she said."

John said, "I think Joses is gonna join you there. It's kinda crowded at Martha and Mary's. How's Sarah? I haven't talked to her since the feast in Cana, like, four months ago."

Matt said, "She seems kind of restless. But she's coming here for the festival at the end of the month. My mom and Jesus' mom and Little James' mom and Concordia's mom and her servant Mina will all be travelling together, and they'll bring my brothers with them."

"That's good. I'll be glad to see her."

Jesus was teaching the crowd among the Colonnades of Solomon. Behind him were his disciples, and behind them was the view of the Mount of Olives, on the other side of the brook Kidron.

Jesus turned around to face his disciples, and said, "Truly I tell you, the kingdom of God is near. You must be ready. Stay dressed for action and keep your lamps burning.

"You must be like servants who are waiting for their master to come home from the wedding feast, so they may open the door right away when he knocks. Blessed are those servants whom the master finds awake when he comes.

"Truly I say that he will dress himself for service. He'll have his servants recline at the table, and he himself will come and serve them. If he comes during the second watch, or at the third watch, and finds them awake, blessed are those servants!

"Look at it this way: If the master of a house knows at what hour the thief is coming, he would stay awake and would not leave the house unguarded to be broken into. In the same way, you must be ready, for the Son of Man is coming at an hour you do not expect."

Peter said, "Lord, is this parable for us or for everyone?"

Jesus said, "Well then, let's see. Who indeed is the faithful and wise manager, the one who will be set over the household to give them their portion of food at the proper time?"

"Blessed is that servant whom his master finds doing these things when he arrives. Truly I tell you, the master will set him as manager over all his possessions.

"But if that servant says to himself, 'My master is coming late,' and begins to beat the other servants, and eat his fill and get drunk, the master of that servant will come on a day that he doesn't expect and an hour he doesn't know, and will cut him in pieces and put him with the unfaithful.

"That servant who knew his master's will but was not ready will get a severe beating. The one who did not know his will and was not ready will receive a light beating.

"To whom much is given, much will be required, and from he who is entrusted with much, yet more will be demanded of him."[87]

52

• •

INTERPRET THE TIMES

John and Thaddeus were standing near Jesus as he taught again in Solomon's Colonnade. Jesus was just warming up, as the crowd grew before him until there were several thousand people listening to him.

Jesus said to the crowd, "I have told you that the kingdom of God is at hand. But some among you say, 'Today is like yesterday, and the day before; where is this "kingdom of God?"'

"But when you see a cloud rising in the west, what do you say right away? You say at once, 'Look, a shower is coming.' And so it happens. And when you see that the south wind is blowing, you say, 'It's going to be hot,' and so it also happens.

"You hypocrites! You claim to know how to interpret the appearance of the earth and the sky, but why don't you know how to interpret the present time?

"The time of trial is near, and you are not ready for the judge. And why don't you judge for yourselves what is right?

"Listen! As you go with your accuser to appear before the magistrate, do your best to settle his claims against you while you are still on the way. If you don't, he will drag you before the judge, and the judge will hand you over to the officer, and the officer will throw you into the prison. I tell you, you will never get out until you have paid the very last lepton." [88]

• • ● • •

John and Thaddeus were walking with Jesus and the rest of the Twelve on the lane leading to Bethany, after they had slipped away from the crowd on the temple grounds.

Thaddeus said, "Teacher, explain to us the parable of the accuser and the magistrate."

Jesus said, "You don't understand this parable? So how will you understand the parable of your life, which presents itself to you every day when you rise?

"The accuser is Satan. He knows each and every wrong thing you have done, for his spirits watch what you do. He takes these complaints to the Father, to present them as proof that you should never enter the kingdom of God, but be consigned instead to himself, to do with you as he wishes.

"As you travel the path of your life, you must always be ready to repent and to ask forgiveness any time that you do wrong to your brother, so that these things will not be held against you.

"The magistrate is the only Son of the Father, who hears these things and will pass judgment. He will separate the sheep from the goats.

"Some he will welcome into the kingdom, but some he will send to the judge to be cast into the prison, which represents everlasting separation from the Father.

"But I tell you truly, there are those who have become faithful followers of the Son of Man. These will not see the judgment, but will be welcomed joyously into the kingdom of the Father."

53

ONE MORE CHANCE

WEDNESDAY, 7 DECEMBER AD 29, 10:00 AM

Someone shouted, "Teacher, what about the Galileans whose blood was mingled with their sacrifices by Governor Pilate?" The crowd murmured, looking for an answer from Jesus.

John strained to see who might have yelled this, but the voice had come from the edge of the crowd and he couldn't pick the man out. But he remembered the news some years back about a riot in the temple, when Roman soldiers had to come in to arrest some Galilean Zealots who were trying to take the temple out of the grip of the Sadducee high priests.[89]

Jesus answered the crowd, "What, do you think that these Galileans were worse sinners than all others, because of what happened to them? I tell you that they were not worse, but unless you repent of your sins, you will die just as they did.

"Or you may tell me about the eighteen men who died when the tower in Siloam fell and killed them. Do you think they were worse sinners than all others living in Jerusalem? I tell you they weren't any worse than the rest of you, but unless you repent, you will die just as they did.

"Therefore hear this: A landholder had a fig tree which was planted in his vineyard, and he came looking for figs, but he found none. So he told his vinedresser, 'Look, for three years now I've come looking for figs on this tree and haven't found any at all. Cut it down; it's just taking up space.'

"The vinedresser answered him, 'Lord, let it grow one more year, and I will cultivate around it and put on fertilizer. Then if it bears figs next year, that will be good. But if not, you can cut it down.'

"Everyone who has ears to hear, let them hear."

<hr>

That night John and Jesus and the rest of the Twelve were around the table at Martha and Mary's house, when John asked, "Teacher, tell us about the parable of the fig tree."

Jesus smiled at them and said, "Ah yes. Well, this is for those of you with wax plugging your ears.

"You heard the questions about the Galileans whose blood was mixed with their sacrifices and the eighteen who died in the fall of the tower in Siloam. There are many people who believe, 'Their sin must be worse than mine; I'm going to be all right for now. I'm not so bad.' But they have not repented of their own sin.

"The fig tree is the person who produces no fruit for the kingdom of God, yet he thinks, 'I am all right for now; there are plenty of other people who are producing fruit.'

"The landholder is the magistrate, who separates the ones who bear fruit from the ones who do not. If no fruit is produced, that plant is thrown into the fire.

"The vinedresser is the Son of Man, who will bring water and the word to the nonproducing people, to give them one more chance to bear fruit. Perhaps they will hear the word and repent, gaining the kingdom. Or perhaps they will cover their ears, and refuse their salvation and the kingdom." [90]

54

Cast Out

Saturday, 10 December AD 29, 8:00 AM

"Wow, Jesus is invited to speak at the Synagogue of Hillel? How'd that happen?"

Little James said, "I'm not sure, John. I think they've been wondering what Jesus is teaching on the temple grounds, but they don't go there because the crowds are too noisy and boisterous."

"This is going to be interesting," said John.

"Yes, and the Twelve are invited to attend as well."

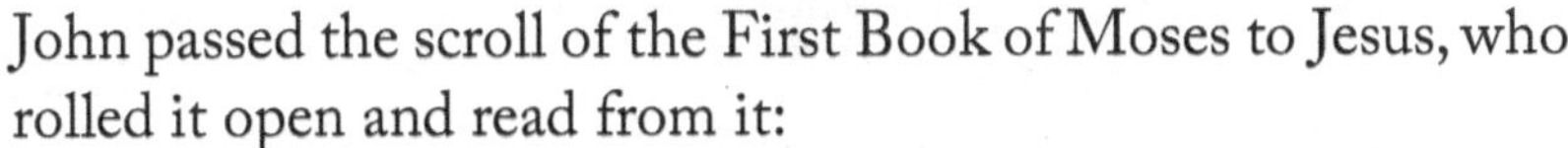

John passed the scroll of the First Book of Moses to Jesus, who rolled it open and read from it:

> The Lord God said, "It is not good for man to be alone. I will make a helper suitable for him." So the Lord God caused a deep sleep to fall upon the man, and as he slept, he took one of his ribs and closed up the man's flesh. The Lord God took the rib and fashioned it into a woman, and brought her to the man.

The man said, "This is now bone of my bones, and flesh of my flesh; she shall be called woman, because this one was taken out of man."

For this reason, a man shall leave his father and mother, and be joined to his wife, and they shall become one flesh.[91]

Jesus gave back the scroll and sat down, and said, "Tell me, if a man and a woman become one flesh, how then can they become two again rather than one?"

A Pharisee stood up and said, "Hillel teaches us that a man can divorce a wife for any and all reasons. But Shammai says that he can only divorce her for a very serious transgression."

Jesus said, "What did Moses command you?"

The Pharisee said, "Moses permitted a man to send his wife away if he first wrote her a certificate of divorce."

Jesus said, "It is only because of the hardness of your hearts that he gave you this permission. But from the beginning God made them male and female. For this reason, a man shall leave his father and mother and the two—the male and the female—shall become one flesh. So they are no longer two, but one flesh. What God has joined together, let no man separate."

James son of Zebedee stood and asked, rather hesitantly, "Does this mean that divorce is always a sin?"

Jesus said, "Whoever divorces his wife in order to marry another woman commits adultery against his wife, and if she herself divorces her husband in order to marry another man, she also is committing adultery."[92]

James and the Pharisee sat down, and the synagogue service continued.

———•••●••·———

After the service, Jesus and John made their way toward the door. But on the way they encountered a woman who was bent over and could not straighten herself. Jesus asked, "Woman, how long have you suffered from this disability?"

She answered, "Eighteen years, my Lord."

Jesus said, "Woman, you are freed from your disability." Jesus laid his hands on her, and immediately she was healed and could straighten up.

She called out joyously, "Oh, glory to God! I'm healed!"

The ruler of the synagogue was right behind Jesus, and he was indignant. He called out in a loud voice, "There are six days in which work should be done. Come on those days and be healed, but not on the Sabbath day!"

Jesus said, "You hypocrites! Won't each of you on the Sabbath untie his ox or his donkey from the manger and lead it away to water? And shouldn't this woman, a daughter of Abraham bound by Satan for eighteen years, be loosed from her bond on the Sabbath?"

Several women in the building said to the ruler of the synagogue, "Shame! Shame on you! Have you no mercy? This man has done glorious things through God!" [93]

Immediately the ruler gathered together the elders in the synagogue, and after a short conversation he called out loudly, "This man that breaks the Sabbath is cast out from this synagogue, along with all of his disciples!"

55

SALT

FRIDAY, 16 DECEMBER AD 29, 3:00 PM

John and Andrew were at the front of the pack of travelers again, followed by the Twelve and the Four, and most of the other fifteen disciples that followed Jesus through Galilee, and a couple dozen newly minted disciples from Jerusalem and its surroundings.

John looked ahead, and it appeared that there was a delegation of about four that were coming to meet them as they approached Amathus in the district of Perea.

As they came closer, one of them called out, "Hello, John!"

John was curious. Who from Amathus would be calling him by name? Then he saw that it was the ruler of the synagogue where Jesus had taught.

"Hello, John," he said again. "Do you think Jesus would consider teaching in our synagogue tonight? Attendance has been down and we're looking to raise some awareness in the sons of Abraham here."

John said, "As a matter of fact, yes. Jesus expressed some interest to me in doing exactly that."

"Wonderful!" he said. "Is there anything I can do for you?"

Andrew said, "Yes, perhaps. We're expecting seventy-two disciples to arrive this week, returning from a mission. We're going to need some lodging for a few days."

"I can help you with that," he said. "See me before the meeting and I will introduce you to some contacts that can provide all the housing you need. And welcome back to our city!"

•••◉•••

Jesus stood up, and John delivered the scroll of Job to him. He unrolled the scroll, found the place, and began to read:

> Job answered his friends and said:
> "Oh, that my grief were actually weighed,
>   and laid in the balances with all my calamity!
> For then it would be heavier than the sand of
>   the sea;
>   therefore my words have been rash.
> For the arrows of the Almighty are in me;
>   my spirit drinks their poison;
>   the terrors of God are arrayed against me.
> Does the wild donkey bray when he has grass,
>   or the ox complain over his fodder?
> Can that which is tasteless be eaten without salt,
>   or is there any taste in the white of an egg?" [94]

Jesus returned the scroll and sat down, and said, "Woe to you who have lost your savor! Woe to you who meet the day with indifference to God!

"The God that created you and divided the sea for you longs for you come back to him. He longs to hear you say, 'I belong to the Lord,' He is waiting for you. Do not make him wait too long.

"You are the salt of the earth, but if salt has lost its taste, how shall its saltiness be restored? What good is tasteless salt? It is useless for the soil or the compost heap. It is good for nothing except to be thrown out and trampled underfoot.

"For everyone will be salted with fire. I say to you, have salt in yourselves, and be at peace with one another. Anyone here who has two good ears, listen up." [95]

As he said these things, a woman in the assembly raised her voice and said, "Blessed is the womb that bore you, and the breasts at which you nursed!"

But Jesus said, "Rather, blessed are those who hear the word of God and keep it!" [96]

Judas *bar* Sabbas poked his head into the door of the inn and said, "Hey Andrew, are you in here?"

Andrew and John came out from an inner room and Andrew said, "I'm here. What's up?"

"Hey, I've already got a couple guys from the seventy-two that have arrived. Did I hear you say that you know where to get more lodging?"

Andrew said, "Yeah, I'll go with you to show you."

Judas said, "These guys are stoked. They can't wait to tell their stories to someone."

John said, "I'll go with you too. I wanna hear this."

56

SEVENTY RETURN

SUNDAY, 19 DECEMBER AD 29, 7:00 AM

Judas *bar* Sabbas knocked on the door of the inn where the Twelve were staying, and Peter answered the door. He said, "Peter! Just the guy I'm looking for. The last two guys from the seventy-two got in last night. We're good to go."

Peter said, "Great! Spread the word, and have everyone meet at the town plaza after breakfast. It's story-telling time!"

John and Matt and Thaddeus were early to the plaza, but it was already filling up with disciples. Some of the townspeople heard the commotion, and came outside to listen to what was going on. Jesus was soon there, and he stood at the very center while the thirty-six pairs of disciples joyously told their stories.

They said, "Lord, even the demons are subject to us in your name!"

Jesus said, "I'll tell you what, I saw Satan fall like lightning from heaven. See, I've given you authority to tread on serpents and scorpions, and over all the power of the enemy. Nothing shall hurt you. Still, don't rejoice that the spirits are subject to you, but rejoice that your names are written in heaven."

When all the stories were told, Jesus rejoiced happily and said, "I thank you, Father, Lord of heaven and earth, that you have hidden these things from the wise and understanding and revealed them to little children. Yes, Father, for so it has pleased you well."

As he said this, he laid one hand on John at his right, and the other hand on Thaddeus at his left.

Then he called loudly to the onlookers, saying, "All things have been given over to me by my Father. No one knows who the Son is except the Father. No one knows who the Father is except the Son, and those to whom the Son chooses to reveal him."

Then turning to the disciples, he tempered his voice and said, "Blessed are the eyes that see what you see! For I tell you that many prophets and kings desired to see what you see, and did not see it, and to hear what you hear, and did not hear it.[97]

"Tomorrow morning, we march on Jerusalem to celebrate the Festival of Lights!"

57

NOT MY SHEEP

WEDNESDAY, 21 DECEMBER AD 29, 6:00 PM

There was a stiff cold breeze blowing across Solomon's colonnade, and John was walking with Jesus and Tad and Matt and Hezekiah. Twenty or thirty of Jesus' disciples were not far behind. They were returning from the temple ritual that lit the first candle of the eight-day celebration.

Many people were there for the first day of the Festival of Lights, but the crowds were thinner than usual because of the stiff breeze.

But there was a group of Pharisees that had noticed Jesus inside the temple, and they had followed him out, along with some of their friends. They gathered around Jesus and one of them said, "How long will you keep us in suspense?"

And another one said, "Yes, if you are the Messiah, tell us now plainly."

Jesus replied, "I already told you, but you do not believe. The works that I do in my Father's name bear witness about me, but you do not believe because you are not my sheep.

"My sheep hear my voice, and I know them, and they follow me. I give them eternal life, and they will never die. No one can snatch them out of my hand.

"My Father who has given them to me is greater than any power, and no one can snatch them out of my Father's hand. I and the Father are one."

Some of them picked up stones to throw at Jesus. The disciples drew in closer.

Jesus said, "I have shown you many good works that come from the Father. Which one of them causes you to stone me?"

One of the Pharisees said, "We're not going to stone you for any good work. We're going to stone you for blasphemy. You're only a man, but you make yourself out to be God."

Jesus said, "Isn't it written in your Law, 'I said, you are gods'? If he to whom the word of God came called them gods—and the scripture cannot be broken—then will you say to the one who the Father consecrated, 'You're blaspheming,' because I said, 'I am the Son of God'?

"If I'm not doing the works of my Father, then don't believe me. But if I am doing them, even though you don't believe me, believe the works. In this way, you can learn that the Father is in me and I am in the Father."

One of the Pharisees said, "Call the temple guard, and tell them to arrest this man."

The disciples moved in more closely around Jesus. Then they separated, and Jesus was no longer there. The Pharisees looked around in confusion, but could not see him anywhere.[98]

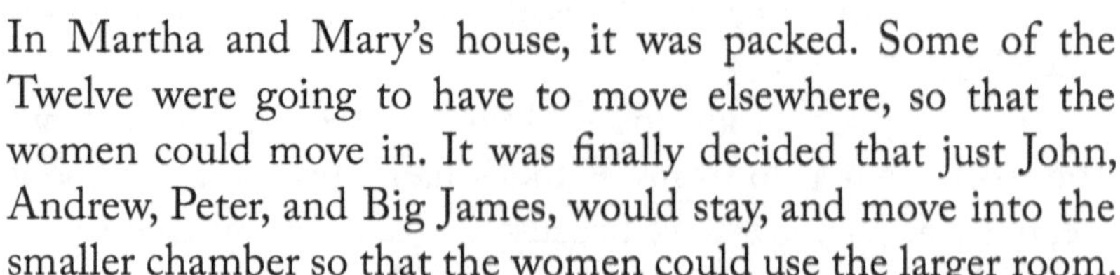

In Martha and Mary's house, it was packed. Some of the Twelve were going to have to move elsewhere, so that the women could move in. It was finally decided that just John, Andrew, Peter, and Big James, would stay, and move into the smaller chamber so that the women could use the larger room.

That was just fine with John. He would have to use Peter as his chaperone, or else Concordia. But Sarah and John could still talk while the crowd was there. They found a corner to sit in, under the watchful eye of Sarah's mom.

John said, "Are you women going to stay for the whole eight days of the festival?"

Sarah said, "It sounds weird when you say, 'you women.' It makes me feel old."

John was embarrassed. He said, "I'm sorry. I just haven't seen you for such a long time."

"I know; it seems like a year went by already. But we'll be here till the last day of the feast."

"Jesus says he's not going back to Galilee."

Sarah winced, and her eyes moistened as if she was going to shed a tear. "That's going to make things tough," she said.

"I know. I don't know what's going to happen. Thomas says we're all gonna die, but I don't believe that. Jesus is in charge, and he has other plans."

"I'm scared."

"Me too. Or at least, I'm scared when I'm not with Jesus. It seems like when he's around, everything's gonna be right. Somehow. But it doesn't make sense."

Sarah broke the tension, saying "I wanna go to that inn where you stayed with Little James. Everybody says the food there is wonderful."

John said, "I'll find a way to make that happen. Maybe go with Peter and Concordia. They haven't been there yet."

Sarah smiled. "I knew you could do it, John."

John smiled too, and leaned back against the wall beside Sarah. For a long time they didn't say anything, while the hubbub and conversations swirled around them. John heard none of it.

58

• •

BETHABARA

FRIDAY, 30 DECEMBER AD 29, 8:00 AM

John and Jesus greeted Abbaquila and he responded in his most hearty voice. "Welcome! We will be enjoying your going-away feast this very night."

Jesus laughed. "I'm looking forward to it. But what are all these houses?"

Abbaquila said, "It has been almost three years since your last going-away party, and we have prospered greatly. When you were here we had five houses, and now we have five more."

Jesus said, "God is rewarding you, my friend."

"I know, and I thank him every day. But what's all this company you bring? Last year you had only five."

"Yes, and this year we are thirteen. These are my closest friends." Jesus laughed. "God knew you were going to need more houses. We may be here a few weeks."

"Party-time at dusk," Abbaquila said, as he turned to go back into his house.

Thomas asked John, "So this is Bethabara?"

John said, "Oh no, this is Bet-Anaya, or in Greek, *Bethany-Beyond-Jordan*. Bethabara is the four houses down at the river crossing. They belong to the people who operate the ferry. I think Abbaquila owns this property."

As the day wore on a trickle of people came into Bet-Anaya looking for Jesus, and remembering the baptisms that John the Baptist did at Bethabara. Jesus greeted them and talked with them when they arrived.

One of the men said, "John didn't perform any powerful signs, but everything that John said about this man Jesus was true."

Another man brought his wife and children to meet "this Jesus" that he'd been hearing about, and after seeing and hearing him, his whole family became believers.[99]

John said to Nate, "I guess there's no place that Jesus can get away to where people won't come looking for him."

Nate answered, "You're right. And it seems like the ones who come to know him end up believing in him."

John said, "I wish that were true in Jerusalem."

Nate said, "That's because they don't want to know him and have closed their eyes and ears."

EPILOGUE

FIRE ON THE EARTH!

SATURDAY, 31 DECEMBER AD 29, 8:00 PM

It was late, but there wasn't any chill wind blowing. Jesus and John had come out to this little hill to pray, and after praying they were just watching the stars.

John said, "Oh look, a shooting star!"

Jesus was quiet.

John said, "It seems so peaceful here, that even a silent star passing through the sky can disturb the peace."

Jesus said, "The star reminds me of why I have come."

John said, "What do you mean?"

Jesus became suddenly intense, saying, "I have come to cast fire on the earth, and I wish that it were already kindled! I have a baptism to be baptized with, and my distress is great until it's accomplished!

"Do you think I've come to bring peace on earth? No, I say, but rather division. From now on, in one house there will be five divided, three against two and two against three.

"They will be divided father against son and son against father, mother against daughter and daughter against mother,

mother-in-law against her daughter-in-law, and daughter-in-law against her mother-in-law."

John was disturbed. He said, "There won't be any peace?"

Jesus said, "For those who will accept it, I bring peace between God and mankind." [100]

NOTES AND SUGGESTED BIBLE READINGS

1. Gehenna means "Valley of Hinnom." It is cursed because of the pagan practices that took place there.

2. Hanukkah.

3. Fort Machaerus on the east bank of the Dead Sea was the capital of Perea, one of Herod Antipas' two kingdoms. His other kingdom was Galilee, and its capital was Tiberias, on the west bank of the Sea of Galilee.

4. John 4:36–54.

5. Luke 7:2–10.

6. Matthew 9:18–19, 23–26; Mark 5:22–24, 35–43; Luke 8:41–42, 49–56.

7. Mk 6:30, Lk 9:10a.

8. *Cf.* Luke 13:31–33, New American Standard Bible (NASB).

9. Here are Jesus' named disciples in the story, both fictional and nonfictional. Nonfictional disciples have a Bible reference.

    1. Simon Peter son of Jonah (John 1:41).
    2. Andrew son of Jonah (John 1:40).
    3. James son of Zebedee (Mark 1:19).

4.   John son of Zebedee (Mark 1:19).
5.   Philip of Bethsaida (John 1:44).
6.   Nathanael (Bartholomew) of Cana (John 1:45).
7.   Matthew (Levi) son of Alpheus (Mark 2:14).
8.   James son of Alpheus (Mark 3:18).
9.   Judas Thaddeus son of James (Mark 3:18).
10.   Thomas, called the Twin (John 11:16).
11.   Simon the Zealot (Luke 6:15).
12.   Judas son of Simon man of Kerioth (John 6:71).
13.   Matthias Justus (Acts 1:23).
14.   Joseph son of Sabbas (Acts 1:23).
15.   Beon—fictional fisherman employee of Peter.
16.   Bohan—fictional fisherman employee of Peter.
17.   Un–named (Concordia) wife of Peter (Mark 1:30).
18.   Mary of Magdala (Luke 8:2).
19.   Susanna (Luke 8:3).
20.   Joanna wife of Chuza (Luke 8:3).
21.   Michael—fictional son of Joanna.
22.   Matt—fictional oldest son of Matthew.
23.   Perez—fictional tax collector, friend of Matthew.
24.   Un-named (Gemariah) disciple (Luke 9:57–58).
25.   Un-named (Tobias) disciple (Luke 9:59–60).
26.   Simon the Leper (Mark 14:3).
27.   Joses son of Alpheus (Mark 15:40).
28.   Daniel—fictional disciple of the Baptist.
29.   Linus—fictional disciple of the Baptist.
30.   Libni—fictional disciple of the Baptist.
31.   Shimei—fictional disciple of the Baptist.
32.   Elnathan—fictional disciple of Nicodemus.
33.   Clopas—friend of Elnathan (Luke 24:18).

[10]   Matthew 14:1–2, Mark 6:14–16, Luke 9:7–9.

[11]   The *haftarah* is a passage from the book of a prophet, read in the synagogue after a passage from one of the Five

Books of Moses. The reading was delivered in the original Hebrew language, and it was customary to comment on it in Aramaic, the language of the people.

12   *Cf.* 2 Samuel 21:15–17 New English Bible.

13   *Cf.* John 5:33,35 English Standard Version (ESV).

14   *Cf.* John 1:6–15 NASB.

15   In Greek, Nathanael was known as Bartholomew (son of Tholmai).

16   *Cf.* Matthew 14:13a, Mark 6:31, John 6:1 ESV.

17   The Jewish month of Nissan started on April 5 in AD 29.

18   Matthew 14:13a.

19   *Cf.* Psalm 104:24–25, 27–29 NASB.

20   *Cf.* Matthew 6:25–33; Luke 12:22–32 NASB.

21   Luke 9:10b.

22   "Anna" is the traditional name of a possible third sister of Jesus. Traditional names of the other sisters are Mary and Salome.

23   *Cf.* Mark 13:10, Matthew 24:14 NASB.

24   *Cf.* Luke 14:26–27 NASB.

25   John 6:4.

26   Matthew 14:13b, Mark 6:33a, Luke 9:11a, John 6:1–2.

27   Matthew 14:14, Mark 6:33b–34, Luke 9:11b, John 6:3.

28   Matthew 14:15–23ab, Mark 6:35–46, Luke 9:11–17, John 6:4–18.

29   Matthew 14:23c–33, Mark 6:47–52, John 6:18–21.

30   Matthew 14: 34–36, Mark 6: 53–56.

31   *Cf.* John 6:22–28, Exodus 16:12–13 ESV.

32 *Cf.* Exodus 16:4, 12–21 ESV.

33 *Cf.* Psalm 78:19–29 ESV.

34 *Cf.* Isaiah 55:1–3 ESV.

35 *Cf.* John 6:28–35, 40 ESV.

36 *Cf.* Isaiah 54:13, John 6:41–45, 48, 56–58 ESV.

37 *Cf.* John 6:60–71 ESV.

38 Matthew 15:21–28, Mark 7:24–30.

39 John 7:1.

40 Matthew 15:29–31, Mark 7:31–37.

41 Matthew 15:32–39, Mark 8:1–10.

42 Matthew 16:1–4, Mark 8:10–13.

43 *Cf.* Mark 8:14–21, Matthew 16:11–12 ESV.

44 Deuteronomy 18:21–22.

45 Mark 8:22–26.

46 Pentecost.

47 The Greek *Christos* (anointed one of God) translates the Aramaic *Messiah* (promised deliverer of the Jewish people).

48 In Greek, *Petros* (Peter) and *petra* (stone) sound similar.

49 Matthew 16:13–20, Mark 8:27–30, Luke 9:18–21.

50 Matthew 16:21–23, Mark 8:31–33, Luke 9:22.

51 *Cf.* Matthew 16:24–28, Mark 8:34–9:1, Luke 9:23–27 ESV.

52 Matthew 17:1–13, Mark 9:2–13, Luke 9:28–36.

53 Matthew 17:14–21, Mark 9:14–29, Luke 9:37–43a.

54 2 Kings 1:8.

55 *Cf.* Matthew 17:22–23, Mark 9:30–32, Luke 9:43b–45 ESV.

56 Matthew 18:1–6, Mark 9:33–37, Luke 9:46–4.

57   *Cf.* Mark 9:38–41 ESV.

58   Luke 9:51.

59   Exodus 20:12, 21:17.

60   Isaiah 29:13.

61   Matthew 15:1–20, Mark 7:1–20.

62   John 7:2–9.

63   Luke 9:52–56, Mark 3:17.

64   *Cf.* Malachi 2:7–9 ESV.

65   Matthew 19:1–2, 18:7–9, Mark 9:43–48.

66   John 7:2, 10–36.

67   Isaiah 44:3.

68   John 7:37–52.

69   Early Christian literature implies that Thomas was a trained architect.

70   Rabbi Hillel did indeed die around AD 10, but the synagogue is fictional.

71   John 9:1–7, 14.

72   *Cf.* John 8:21–59 ESV.

73   *Cf.* John 9:8–41 ESV.

74   Ezekiel 34:1–5, 11–12 ESV.

75   *Cf.* John 10:1–9, 14–18, 21 ESV.

76   Luke 9:61–62.

77   *Cf.* Luke 10:1–12, 16 ESV.

78   Isaiah 60:15.

79   Luke 10:25–29.

80   *Cf.* Luke 10:29–37 ESV.

81   Luke 10:38–42.

82   Luke 11:1–13, Matthew 6:5–15.

83   Luke 11:37–54.

84   A lepton is a Jewish coin worth about four minutes of a laborer's daily wage.

85   *Cf.* Luke 12:1–12 ESV.

86   *Cf.* Luke 12:13–34 ESV.

87   *Cf.* Luke 12:35–48 ESV.

88   *Cf.* Luke 12:54–59 ESV.

89   History is silent about this incident with Pilate, but a similar incident is recorded under a previous governor.

90   Luke 13:1–9.

91   *Cf.* Genesis 2:18, 21–24 NASB.

92   Mark 10:1–12.

93   Luke 13:10–17.

94   Job 6:1–6 NASB.

95   Mt 5:13, Mk 9:49–50, Lk 14:34.

96   Luke 11:27–28 ESV.

97   *Cf.* Luke 10:17–24 ESV.

98   *Cf.* John 10:22–39 ESV.

99   John 10:40–42.

100   *Cf.* Luke 12:49–53 ESV.

Thank you for taking the time to read *John and the Jesus Boat Episode Three*. I hope you've been delighted by John as much as I've been delighted to share him with you. Episode Three is the third of a four-episode series that follows the life of teenage Apostle John through his appearances in the Bible. Here is a sneak preview from *Episode Four: AD 30 – A New Hope*.

"Mother Mary! It's good to see you. How are you?"

"I'm doing well in my health, John, but I'm in sorrow for my son Jesus."

"Oh, why, Mother? What's wrong?"

"Jesus says he won't be returning to Galilee, and I fear for him. I thought I was well settled with Peter's mother-in-law in Capernaum, but now I want to move closer to Jerusalem. On the other hand, I don't want to rent a house there all by myself. I would get lonely."

"Oh, I hope you find a way. I wish I could help. What will you do now?"

"That's lovely of you, John. For now, I'm thinking of moving to Ephraim and staying with the Alpheus family. Joses' and Little James' mother is the only woman there and she would like some company, I think."

John said, "That's still twenty miles from Jerusalem. But it's workable as a day's journey."

"Yes, John, but I'm not getting any younger."

"I will pray for you, mother Mary."

John and the Jesus Boat Episode Four: AD 30—A New Hope is in work and you can get it first at amazon.com. You're also invited to "like" my author page at Facebook.com/AuthorRolinBruno to get the latest publishing schedule. Tell a friend!

Rolin Bruno
January, AD 2019